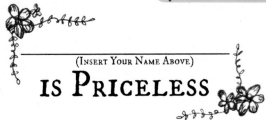

(INSERT YOUR NAME ABOVE)

is PRICELESS

But now, God's Message,
the God who made you in the first place, Jacob,
   the One who got you started, Israel:
"Don't be afraid, I've redeemed you.
   I've called your name. You're mine.
When you're in over your head, I'll be there with you.
   When you're in rough waters, you will not go down.
When you're between a rock and a hard place,
   it won't be a dead end—
Because I am God, your personal God,
   The Holy of Israel, your Savior.
I paid a huge price for you:
   all of Egypt, with rich Cush and Seba thrown in!
That's how much you mean to me!
   That's how much I love you!
I'd sell off the whole world to get you back,
   trade the creation just for you."
                  —Isaiah 43:1–4 (MSG)

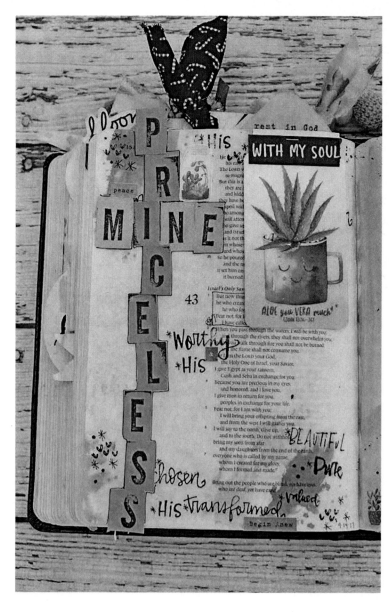

You are PRICELESS

SARAH MALANOWSKI

*Along with 22 women who have experienced
the power of redemption in Jesus Christ.*

Dedicated to every woman who has a redemption story. May the power of your testimony in Jesus Christ never be stifled by the enemy's attacks of shame or guilt. You are an overcomer! You are radiant and beautiful because the One who loves you, bought you, and actually made you priceless through His precious blood!

Acknowledgments

Thank You God for the extreme honor of bringing this book together. Thank You for every testimony You brought in and the blessing we have to glorify You with what You have entrusted to us!

Thank you Paul, my hubby, for your constant encouragement in this endeavor, for believing in me, and never letting me quit!

Thank you Zion and Gabriel, my precious boys, for sharing your mommy with those who have yet to know the hope found in Jesus Christ!

Thank you Joyce Kelly for all that you did to help me bring this together! I couldn't have done this without you. I'm blessed to have you as my spiritual mentor!

Thank you to the ladies who entrusted their testimonies to me for this book! Thank you Christa Hernandez, Ivory Granger, Jennifer Werle, Christine Batsell, Denise Horne, Kathy Cunningham, Brandee Nielsen Smith, Kirsten Voorhees, Mona Giordano, Dominique Richardson, Jayne Solomon, Deborah Yoerg, Joyce Kelly, Kim Thomas, Cole Ian, Erin Blair, Cheryl Moore, Julie Koster, Angie Rodriguez, Heather Richmond, Dotti Groover-Skipper, and Stephanie. I can't wait to hear how God will use our testimonies to advance His glory and provide freedom to those who still find themselves enslaved by thoughts of the enemy.

Thank you to the ladies who provided Scripture art for the book. Thank you Keisha Polonio, Sammy Esquivel, Jessica Serrano, Karissa Birberick, Jana Gatlyn, Krystal Whitten, Julie Higgins, Isabella Moore, and Maddie Fabian. Your talent and ability truly amaze me and it's a gift to have it represented in this book!

Thank you to Kim Huther for all of your edits on this book and for helping me look smart in the process!

Thank you Kimberly McClure for your beautiful design work in this book! It's been a privilege to work with you and the skills that you have to bring the vision in my mind to life. This book looks amazing because of the time and effort you spent on it!

THE ...LORD... HIMSELF

will

>>>Fight-For→You←≪

= Just stay calm. =

·:EXODUS 14:14:·

KPulomo

God has been writing this book in Sarah Malanowski's heart for years. Like Nehemiah, Sarah refused to come down off the wall when the Sanballats of the world were calling her to drop her pen and to desert her dream. She wouldn't come down because she knew the wall God wanted to build was going to be a wall of safety, protection, and security for many whose walls have fallen and whose lives have fallen apart. Today there are 1.6 million homeless and runaway children in America. Within hours of them dropping off the radar, thousands of them will be sex-trafficked, a polite term for being repeatedly raped. Today, with the ongoing fight of a political and legal system, it seems voices are needed for those who have no voice. And when they're rescued, who will speak for them and who will speak into them? Sarah Malanowski, that's who.

The Bible says the thief does not come except to steal, to kill, and to destroy (John 10:10). We know the thief is Satan who steals purity, kills possibilities, and destroys potentiality. *You Are Priceless* is a reminder to each victim that while the thief is strong and purposes to ruin, we have a Living Savior who is stronger and who purposes to redeem, restore, and rescue with a promise. He said, "I have come that they may have life and that they may have it more abundantly." (John 10:10b, NKJV)

This book has one purpose...to give Hope. Every devotion, every testimony, is meant to speak to the heart of the broken, downcast person who only sees where her heels have been and not where her toes are pointed. *You Are Priceless* tells you, because of the great *"I AM," you are Priceless – Free – Precious – Loved – Treasured – Beautiful – Worthy – Enough – Wanted – and Safe.*

God gave us a great promise in Isaiah 61. He said when Jesus Christ comes, He will do some special things for all of us. He declared in Isaiah 61:1-3 NKJV, "I will send Him to heal the brokenhearted, to proclaim liberty to the captives, and the opening of the prison to those who are bound. To comfort all who mourn in Zion, (and I love this one) to give them beauty for ashes, the oil of joy for mourning, the garment of praise for the spirit of heaviness." What a great promise!

That's what this book is meant to do – to help those who are broken, bound, beaten up, and beaten down. These are testimonies from people who have been there, done that, and bought the shirt. Except this time, their shirt says in big, bold letters: "**I Am Priceless!**"

As you read this book and pass it along, please know I am praying for you that God will restore hope, and you will regain the value God intends for you to have. Remember this: when God buried all your sins and mine, He threw them into the sea of forgiveness and put up a sign – "No fishing allowed." All of us have sinned. But let's be very clear about one thing. Those who have been trafficked are victims, and they did not get there because of their sin, but someone else's sin.

Not only may this book give you grace to be healed and restored, but also give you grace to forgive those who have hurt you. Remember, bitterness is an acid that does more damage to the vessel in which it is stored than to the victim on which it is poured.

Always remember, **You Are Priceless**. God bankrupted Heaven for you! He is I AM so you can be YOU ARE. Thank you, Sarah. It is my joy to be your pastor – and I think you are Priceless!

In Him,
Ken Whitten
Senior Pastor
Idlewild Baptist Church
Lutz, Florida

CONTENTS

The Lord
YOUR GOD
goes with you,
HE WILL NOT FAIL YOU

or forsake you.

Deut 31:6

Hello my dear Priceless One,

Do you ever wonder if there's more? Have you ever felt ashamed, unworthy, or insignificant? You, my dear one, are not alone, as many of us have faced these very same questions. In fact, that's the reason for this book. I have invited my comrades in Christ to share how God has taken their moments of insignificance, shame, feelings of unworthiness, and brokenness to express some of His most beautiful work! Then I wrote six devotionals from a biblical perspective, giving insight to how Eve, the woman at the well, Mary Magdalene, and a few others can relate to us as well.

Yes, God is at work. The fact that you have this book in your hands and are reading it confirms how much He loves you. God loves you so much that He specifically designed a moment in time where your path would cross that of the one who handed this to you or made you aware it. God was thinking of you! He's always been thinking of you. He's never stopped loving you!

You are seen! You are known! You are loved! That's the message we hope to portray and we hope you will embrace as you read through these pages. Each part of this book was designed with you in mind. We want you to know that, no matter where you are or what you've done, you are loved! You are deeply treasured by God. He knows each and every tear you've cried, every pain you've endured, and the daily things you go through. Your struggles are the burdens of His heart. There's absolutely nothing you could do to make God love you any more than He already does. Yes, you're loved right where you are! **You Are Priceless,** my dear!

As you read through this book, you will notice we chose different trade taglines in our devotionals. We chose these because we've learned that we can give God our greatest pains, and in return He gives us something beautiful. He wants to take those things that hurt you and burden you and give you His goodness in place of it. We've experienced this first hand as we've traded in our weaknesses for His strength. We've made the trade! Will you? As you read through this devotional and reflect on each trade, please remember:

His banner over you is love. —Song of Solomon 2:4

We have also placed different "I am" statements at the end of each devotional to speak into your life. We did this to remind you of who you truly are. Please look into the mirror while reading these statements of truth. Take the time to replace the lies you've believed and that have been spoken over you in life. We know that, as you claim each truth, you'll experience change and the chains in your life will be broken. May you truly taste and see that the Lord is good as you discover His heart for you!

As you walk through this book, dwell on the "You are..." words that are highlighted at the beginning of each devotional. Embrace the fact that you are priceless, worthy, loved, cherished, and adored! **You, my dear, are absolutely beautiful, one of a kind, and there's no one like you in the whole world.** May you come to treasure how truly unique you are, and that in this life you have a purpose way beyond what you could possibly imagine!

May each devotional help you discover a part of yourself that may have been lost. May you come to understand how truly priceless you are to the King of Kings. Your story, my story, and the stories of those represented in this book are very similar. We all need a

Savior! Not one of us is without sin. Not one of us can say we have it all together. Not one of us can claim that we're perfect. We serve a perfect God, who gave us a perfect Savior.

He gave us a perfect Savior because, from the beginning of time, sin separated us from His holiness. There was a moment in a garden that changed everything. It all started with Eve. You and I are a lot more like her than we think sometimes. We, too, desire more than what we see around us. We, too, struggle with pride and insecurity. We, too, are looking for a place where we belong. We, too, desire to have purpose in this life. We, too, fall prey to the enemy's lies, and end up dead inside from believing them.

My hope is, as you read through this book, that God will show you where you've allowed the lies of the enemy to take root and help you replace them with His Truth. Please use the Scriptures mentioned in this book to meditate upon God's goodness and learn about His character. We serve a God who desires to use our mishaps for His glory. May you come to see just how beautiful the testimonies are that God has entrusted to you, and may you grow in courage to share them boldly. Who knows, your testimony just may be the link to someone experiencing Jesus!

With Love from your Priceless Ambassador,

Sarah

Let
all who take
Refuge
IN YOU
Rejoice
let them SING
For Joy

Psalm 5:11

You are UNIQUE

Therefore, just as sin came into the world through one man, and death through sin, so death spread to all people [no one being able to stop it or escape its power], because they all sinned.

—Romans 5:12 (AMP)

TRADE YOUR DEFICIENCY FOR HIS ABUNDANCE

I was unique. I was one of a kind. I had a beautiful garden to roam in. I had everything I could possibly need, but still I wanted more. I didn't know I wanted more until the enemy came in his oh so cunning way. I should have known when the first words out of his mouth were, "Did God really say…" (Genesis 3:1, NIV) Let me just be clear, if you ever hear the enemy say these words, run for dear life. He's about to bring you down a road of destruction.

At first, I stood my ground and clarified what God really said, to my enemy. But as I dwelled on the thought of being more like God, I slowly felt myself lose my grip. In a moment, I gave in. I took a bite of the fruit that God forbade me to have. One moment of sin forever changed the trajectory of my life, and the lives of those who came after me. That moment of sin stole everything away from me, yet God came back for me. He came back for a walk with me, but my sin separated me from His holiness. Still, He was gracious with me. He clothed me and gave me a place to live with Adam. He didn't abandon me. He didn't give up on me. In fact, He made it known that sin would be crushed for good one day.

"And I will put enmity between you and the woman, and between your offspring and hers; he will crush your head, and you will strike his heel."

—Genesis 3:15 (NIV)

God will get the last word. In fact, I hear that He already has. Listen, it's not too late for you to experience a relationship with the Father. I can testify how good it was to walk in uninterrupted fellowship with Him. There's nothing like it in the world. I let my sin get in the way of that beautiful relationship, but you don't have to. God has sent His Son to take care of your sin once and for all.

We each have a unique story, talents, and gifts. We each have been given a unique way to serve our King. But there is something very similar among us as well. We all battle insecurity. We all battle pride. In our sinful natures, we all think there has to be something more, and then we dance with the devil while we try to find it. Can I just say that there is no sin you could commit that would keep God from loving you? Trust me on this: I was the first one to sin and yet God came back for me. I started this whole sin problem, yet God still gave me the promise of His Son to look forward to. May you see your sin, your brokenness, your weakness as an opportunity to glorify the One who made you. May you testify of His goodness, so that others can experience what it's like to serve a living God who cares and never gives up on you!

This is the kind of love we are talking about—not that we once upon a time loved God, but that he loved us and sent his Son as a sacrifice to clear away our sins and the damage they've done to our relationship with God. —1 John 4:10

Dear Father God, thank You for making a way for me to have fellowship with You. Thank You for not counting my sins against me but for coming after me. Thank You for pursuing me even when I was still ugly and had nothing to offer. Thank You for entrusting to me a testimony that can and will advance Your glory.

I AM UNIQUE. GOD LOVES ME AND HAS A GREAT PLAN FOR MY LIFE. HE WILL USE MY WEAKNESS TO ADVANCE HIS STRENGTH. HE WILL USE MY BROKENNESS TO REVEAL HIS WHOLENESS. HE WILL DO A BEAUTIFUL WORK IN MY LIFE. TODAY, I WILL TRADE MY DEFICIENCY FOR HIS ABUNDANCE. I AM PRICELESS!

(Written by Sarah Malanowski, from the perspective of Eve in Genesis 3:1-15.)

But because of His great

Love

for us, God, who is

Rich in mercy

made us alive with Christ
even when we were

dead

in transgressions, it is by

Grace

you have been

Saved

Ephesians 2:4-5

I'll show up and take care of you as I promised and bring you back home. I know what I'm doing. I have it all planned out—plans to take care of you, not abandon you, plans to give you the future you hope for.

—Jeremiah 29:11

TRADE YOUR HOPELESSNESS FOR HIS PROMISES

Sweet friend let me share with you. Things started bad for me in childhood where I suffered physical, mental, and sexual abuse. At 19, I entered the strip club in hopes to provide for my daughter. I will never forget how I felt walking on stage my first time, but I think the worst was when I had to do my first private dance. I walked away feeling instantly shamed and dirty for what went down during that dance.

A girl in the club befriended me and started giving me drugs, which made what I was doing a lot easier. She then asked me to start driving her, and before I knew it I found out she was a recruiter for who would become my trafficker. I crossed lines I never thought I would. The more lines I crossed, the more worthless I felt. Everything was a transaction, me for money. I began to think this life was all I was good for. I was addicted to drugs, in and out of jail, and even lost my kids at one point. I got away from this trafficker but went back to many other bosses on my own. I didn't know anything else. I was hopeless, and this life had me for twenty years.

At 35, I was invited to church. My first thought was NO WAY; Jesus wants nothing to do with me, I am too dirty. But I went ahead and said yes. Friend, when I walked in that church Jesus grabbed a hold of me and He was the best thing I've ever experienced. My life began to change. At 37, I left the industry with no job experience and still addicted to drugs. He took care of every detail. He showed me I was priceless. He turned my pain into my purpose, and I now go into the clubs to love on the precious ladies there.

You, my dear one, are priceless, too. There is One who has cared for you since the moment you were conceived and He wants nothing more than to lavishly pour out His love on you!

God is telling you, "I've never quit loving you and never will. Expect love, love, and more love!"

—Jeremiah 31:3

Dear Jesus, I pray for a revelation of Your love for me! Lord, please allow me to see You working in my life and restore the vision of Your promises for me. Please fill me with hope and give me the courage to follow Your lead. Help me to trust You with every ounce of my being. In Jesus' name, Amen.

I AM PRICELESS. I AM WORTH FAR MORE THAN RUBIES
AND PEARLS. I AM LOVED BY A PERFECT FATHER RIGHT
WHERE I AM. I HAVE VALUE AND WORTH AND
GOD HAS A GREAT PLAN FOR MY LIFE.
MY CIRCUMSTANCES DON'T DEFINE ME.
TODAY, I WILL TRADE MY HOPELESSNESS
FOR HIS PROMISES.

I AM PRICELESS!

Fearfully
and
Wonderfully
Made

PSALM 139:14

Before I shaped you in the womb, I knew all about you. Before you saw the light of day, I had holy plans for you: a prophet to the nations—that's what I had in mind for you.

—Jeremiah 1:5

TRADE YOUR FAILURE FOR HIS WORTH

Failure. That was a sentiment that I could easily relate to, because that's constantly how I felt when it came to my relationship with my father. I was never good enough. There was always something that I needed to do better. It was stifling, and even debilitating at times. I lived my life striving for perfection, while feeling so insignificant.

I would be so excited about something I was sure he'd be proud of, only to be crushed by the blow of his disdain. I would put on a smile and for the sake of those around me act like my heart wasn't being shredded by the lie that I was worthless, unacceptable, a failure, and a complete waste. But as I grew up, I started taking to heart what God's Word said about me, that no matter how inferior or insignificant I felt, the God of the universe was preparing me for a master plan of His intricate design.

My sweet friend, the same can be said for you today. No matter what anyone has said about you, no matter how much of a failure you've felt like, no matter how insignificant you may feel, God is at work and has a plan designed specifically for you. Before you were even formed in your mother's womb, He had holy plans for you.

As you read this, know that God created you on purpose, for a purpose. He's orchestrated your life, and desires to not only use the good parts, but even the painful, ugly places for His glory. He wants to make beauty from ashes and show the world His beautiful, loved, and cherished masterpiece: *You.*

Today, will you join me in accepting the fact that you matter? That you were made on purpose. That you are so incredibly valuable and have tremendous worth. That God wants to use you and your story in HIStory {His story}! That He's had you in His heart and in His mind before you were even in existence.

Like an open book, you watched me grow from conception to birth; all the stages of my life were spread out before you, the days of my life all prepared before I'd even lived one day.
—Psalm 139:15–16

Dear God, at times it's hard to quiet the thoughts, memories, and experiences that tell me I'm worthless or that I don't matter. Lord, help me to remember that before I was even born You had a purpose and plan for my life and that no one and nothing can steal it away. Please show me how to walk in the plans You have for me.

I AM SIGNIFICANT. I HAVE PURPOSE.
I AM VALUABLE. I AM WORTHY.
I AM ACCEPTED.
I AM GOD'S MASTERPIECE.
TODAY, I WILL TRADE MY FAILURE FOR HIS WORTH.

I AM PRICELESS!

ANYONE *who belongs* to *Christ* has BECOME a *new person.* THE OLD LIFE *is gone;* *a new life has* BEGUN!

II Corin 5:17

"Come. Sit down. Let's argue this out." This is God's Message: "If your sins are blood-red, they'll be snow-white. If they're red like crimson, they'll be like wool."

—Isaiah 1:18

TRADE YOUR DESPAIR FOR HIS HOPE

Growing up, a bright future was in my sights. Then, life happened. Unforeseen events rocked my world and eliminated any sense of 'normalcy.' Alcohol worked for a while, until it wasn't enough. My sister turned me on to hard drugs at 22. I finally had an escape, a way to numb all the intense emotional pain I'd suffered. My heart hurt and when I injected that heroin for the first time, there was no longer any pain. It was the feeling I thought I had been searching for my entire life.

Of course that feeling didn't last long. Before I knew it, I was injecting 20 bags a day just to keep the sickness away. The initial sense of euphoria faded so quickly. So, I started injecting cocaine, cocaine and heroin mixed, crushed up pharmaceuticals, methamphetamines, horse tranquilizers, liquid morphine, and the list goes on. Used them all until my body was used to them, until my former self was nowhere to be found. I was dancing with the devil in the darkness, and there was no light to be found.

After the seventh rehab attempt, and 98 days in jail, I found the light. It was like God flipped a switch, and I was restored. The Word of God was satisfying truth amidst so many lies. The light of Christ came back into my heart and illuminated every single dark and dingy place. That feeling I longed for in the midst of my affliction, was the incomparable peace of Jesus Christ. No counterfeit would do; Christ alone was the healing balm that my soul desperately needed.

You are not the things you have done. You have no control over the bad things that have happened to you in the past. This life has no shortage of things that make our hearts hurt, but God is there, through it all, even when it doesn't feel like it. The price Jesus paid at the cross to cleanse you of your sin was the ultimate sacrifice. There is no realization greater than this. Will you accept His forgiveness and experience the freedom He offers?

Therefore, if anyone is in Christ, he is a new creation. The old has passed away; behold, the new has come.

—2 Corinthians 5:17 (ESV)

Dear Abba Father, Your forgiveness does not even make sense to me. It is beyond my comprehension. Thank You for wiping the slate clean. I can approach You daily without any guilt or shame. Thank You for declaring me holy and blameless, 100% righteous!

I AM FREE AND FORGIVEN.

I AM LOVED BEYOND MY COMPREHENSION.

I AM CHOSEN AND REDEEMED.

TODAY, I WILL TRADE MY DESPAIR FOR HIS HOPE.

I AM PRICELESS!

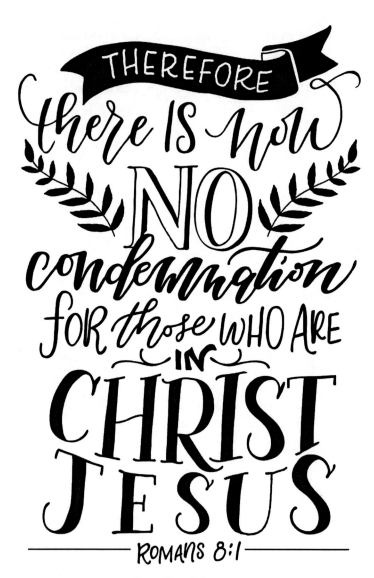

THEREFORE there is now NO condemnation for those WHO ARE IN CHRIST JESUS

ROMANS 8:1

©www.Krystalwhitten.com

You are PRECIOUS

Oh yes, you shaped me first inside, then out; you formed me in my mother's womb... You know me inside and out, you know every bone in my body; you know exactly how I was made, bit by bit, how I was sculpted from nothing into something. Like an open book, you watched me grow from conception to birth; all the stages of my life were spread out before you, the days of my life all prepared before I'd even lived one day.

—Psalm 139:13, 15, & 16

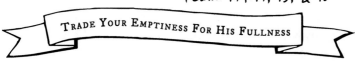

TRADE YOUR EMPTINESS FOR HIS FULLNESS

One of my earliest memories, which is so vivid to me even to this day, is when I was four years old, begging my dad not to leave. "Please, Daddy; please, Daddy, don't go." Years went on and life went on. Unfortunately, I became the victim of molestation at the hand of my own cousins and later I was raped by someone I thought I could trust. The humiliation and shame I felt was truly painful. I learned to suppress those thoughts and live in denial as my personality is to live happy and keep pressing on.

I began feeling like it was love I had been missing. Surely, this was the very thing that could fill the emptiness in my life. I was so obsessed with the things I thought were fulfilling me and happiness that I fooled myself into thinking sex was the answer. I eventually got pregnant. My fear and shame as well as the young man I was dating at the time pushed me to choose abortion. I remember it like it was yesterday.

I sat looking around nervously and fearfully at all the young women in the waiting area who had chosen this path too. We were all scarred girls thinking this was the only answer and acting as if there was no consequence to our actions. The doctor called my name and led me into a typical patient room where I sat up on the table and put my feet in stirrups. They put me to sleep and began to suction my baby out. I woke up in a chair, feeling disoriented, and looking around at those same women who were waking up from their abortions as well. It was a tough day to say the least.

I can tell you from my personal journey that I knew our Heavenly Father had forgiven me of my sin, but I had not forgiven myself. I carried that guilt and pain for 15 years until I accepted God's forgiveness. Do you know that God has forgiven you, too? There is nothing you have done that He can't forgive. You are absolutely precious to Him, and He loves you so much.

He forgives your sins—every one. He heals your
diseases—every one. He redeems you from hell—saves
your life! He crowns you with love and mercy—a
paradise crown. He wraps you in goodness—beauty
eternal. He renews your youth—you're always young
in his presence.

—Psalm 103:3–5

Heavenly Father, thank You for freeing me from my pain,
emptiness, guilt, and shame. I love You, Lord, and desire to be
transformed, renewed, and used to bring others to know You.
Thank You, Lord for taking this broken little girl and turning
her into the beautiful daughter You designed her to be.

I AM PRECIOUS TO GOD. HE HAS FORGIVEN ME.

HE KNOWS ME AND HE CARES FOR ME.

TODAY, I WILL TRADE MY EMPTINESS FOR HIS FULLNESS.

I AM PRICELESS!

When you WALK THROUGH THE Waters I WILL BE THERE & through the Flames you won't be Burned

ISAIAH 43:2

Jerusalem will be told: "Don't be afraid. Dear Zion, don't despair. Your God is present among you, a strong Warrior there to save you. Happy to have you back, He'll calm you with his love and delight you with his songs."

—Zephaniah 3:16—17

TRADE YOUR PAIN FOR HIS LOVE

There are times I can remember wondering, "How could someone love me if my own mom doesn't love me?" Times when I recall the chaos of childhood and all that it entailed. Brokenness was the tale of our home. It was a story familiar to many. Childhood is hard and it sets us up for life. As the day-to-day battles of living with someone who was bi-polar ensued, I remember walking on eggshells thinking, "When will the next explosion happen?"

The day could be going well and out of nowhere a bomb would let off. One of those moments that left you dumbfounded and scrambling for safety. The shrapnel was scattered among the home, leaving gaping wounds for us kids to recover from. Often, I would think to myself, "I'm not worthy. I'm not good enough. If I would have only done such-and-such, maybe this wouldn't have happened." There, in the midst of my pain, God would show up. He loved me and His love was bigger than my pain.

You see, no matter where you are, and no matter what kind of pain you have faced, I can promise God knows it. He sees you. He cares for you! He loves you more than you can imagine. There is absolutely nothing you can do to separate yourself from His love when you accept His Son Jesus as your Savior.

Today, I encourage you to hand your pain over to the One Who has always loved you. The One Who knew you and formed you in your mother's womb. There is not a detail about you that wasn't designed by the Father. Details of excellence! Details of beauty! You are loved, you are cherished, and the King of Kings rejoices over you. I invite you to trade your pain for His love today.

God told them, "I've never quit loving you and never will. Expect love, love, and more love!"

—Jeremiah 31:3

Dear Father God, it's hard to imagine that You love me just as I am and difficult to comprehend that You have never stopped loving me. Lord, please help me embrace this love that You offer. Please teach me what it means to be loved, cherished, and treasured by You. Today, I embrace who You are and accept the love that You give me.

I AM LOVED. I AM CHERISHED.
I AM TREASURED BY THE KING OF KINGS.
I AM ACCEPTED AND WANTED BY THE
ONE WHO DESIGNED MY VERY BEING.
TODAY, I WILL TRADE MY PAIN FOR HIS LOVE.
I AM PRICELESS!

I came that they may have

life;

have it abundantly!

John 10:10

Do this because you are a people set apart as holy to God, your God. God, your God, chose you out of all the people on Earth for himself as a cherished, personal treasure.

—Deuteronomy 7:6

TRADE YOUR GUILT FOR HIS MERCY

Do you know what it's like to lead a double life? I do; I did it most of my life. In high school, I was blessed to be a "popular" girl, but back at home, my house was run by perfectionism, stress, anxiety, as well as verbal and physical abuse. I grew up feeling that failure was not an option. No matter my level of effort, nothing was ever good enough. I started working at age 15 to get out of the house. For most of my childhood I walked on eggshells never knowing if it was going to be a good day. I couldn't wait to grow up! It took more time than I would have liked but by age 21, I'd had enough and moved out. I finally left behind those feelings of dejection and despair.

Unfortunately, my newfound freedom didn't turn out the way I had expected. Within six months I had gone through my savings, but I refused to give up and go back home. I picked up a third job to stay afloat but my grades began to slip. A coworker of mine knew my situation and mentioned a new high-end strip club opening up in the area. Despite my apprehension, I agreed to check it out with her. After one attempt I was hooked. I thought life would be so much easier if I only had one job. I kept trying to rationalize the guilt that I felt and told myself that I would only do what was necessary.

Eventually I lost my way and stopped talking myself out of it, mixing in alcohol to drown out the guilt while being seduced by the glamour. That became my life for the next five years. It was the rock-bottom of my double life, as my family had no idea what I was doing, and I was always pretending to be somebody else when I was dancing.

By age 27, I was tired of feeling guilty and depressed over my past. The only thing that pulled me through was my faith in Jesus Christ. I was led to return to the church where I recommitted my life to my Lord and Savior. Three years later, God blessed me abundantly with a wonderful husband, someone I could finally show my true self to, and then later, two beautiful children. I look back at those tough times in my twenties as a dream instead of a nightmare. I'm thankful that God rescued me from my desperation.

Have you ever felt desperate? Do you know that in your most desperate times, God is there? He sees you. He loves you. He has a plan for you. You can reach out to Him!

Anyone who goes through me will be cared for—will freely go in and out, and find pasture. A thief is only there to steal and kill and destroy. I came so they can have real and eternal life, more and better life than they ever dreamed of.

—John 10:9–10

Dear Father God, I cry out to You in my desperation and I know You hear me. Your love is my constant comfort and in You I experience true, real, and lasting life.

I AM TREASURED.

I AM ADORED BY THE KING OF KINGS.

I AM LOVED AND CHERISHED

BY THE ONE WHO KNOWS ME BEST.

TODAY, I WILL TRADE MY GUILT FOR HIS MERCY.

I AM PRICELESS!

psalms 62:5

LET ALL

THAT I AM

WAIT

quietly

BEFORE

God

FOR

my HOPE
is in

HIM

are

HOPEFUL

We can rejoice, too, when we run into problems and trials, for we know that they help us develop endurance. And endurance develops strength of character, and character strengthens our confident hope of salvation. And this hope will not lead to disappointment. For we know how dearly God loves us, because he has given us the Holy Spirit to fill our hearts with his love.

—Romans 5:3–5 (NLT)

TRADE YOUR SORROW FOR HIS DELIGHT

The situation in my life that has caused me the most grief is the same situation that has caused me to have the strength and perseverance that I have now. As I watched someone I loved more than my own life slowly destroy their life with drugs, I felt a sense of loss and grief that was more than I thought I could bear.

The really hard thing about addiction is that unless you have experienced it yourself or through someone very close to you, you don't understand. So as I journey through my life as someone who has watched addiction take everything away from someone I love, there have been many times I have felt very alone. Yes, my friends and family have tried to be there but in reality they just can't be; they can't understand.

But every time I have felt alone and afraid I would sense God was with me; I was not alone and I did not need to be afraid. In fact, He tells us that these difficult times that seem overwhelming will actually strengthen us and grow our character. But most of all we can look to our God with *hope* that can only come from Him and will not disappoint us. Hope for a future, that God will restore the things we have lost, and provide a peace that surpasses all understanding.

If you are reading this and feel alone or afraid, I want you to know that you have a Father God Who knows and sees your situation. He loves you. He is with you. He will provide for you; you can put your *hope* in Him and that hope will not disappoint.

God, the one and only— I'll wait as long as he says. Everything I hope for comes from him, so why not? He's solid rock under my feet, breathing room for my soul, an impregnable castle: I'm set for life.

—Psalm 62:5–6

Dear Father God, sometimes I feel so alone and afraid. At times, I've felt so hopeless. Please help me to remember that You are the Rock beneath my feet. Today I give You all my fears and declare that You my Father God are always with me. I am never alone.

I AM HOPEFUL. I AM CHERISHED.
I AM PROTECTED. I AM LOVED BY GOD.
TODAY, I WILL TRADE MY
SORROW FOR HIS DELIGHT.
I AM PRICELESS!

For HE WILL ORDER HIS *angels* to Protect you WHEREVER you go

psalm 91:11

You are SHIELDED

But you, God, shield me on all sides; you ground my feet, you lift my head high.

—Psalm 3:3

When I think about the day I sexually gratified another human being in exchange for driving me to safety, I recall how God rescued me, and I'm swept away in a tide of peace.

When I was 15 years old, I loved horseback riding. My dad's boss owned a horse ranch and invited me to spend a weekend riding with his daughter. The plan was to go to work with my dad, where his boss would pick me up. I said goodbye to my dad as we drove off in a van. When I noticed the direction we were heading crossed the state line, my heart began to pound! I realized I had just been kidnapped, and I silently prayed for God to save me. During the next few hours, I was subjected to conversations about older men having sex with young girls, and attempts to get me intoxicated with alcohol.

Though I was frightened, I held firm to my faith that God would save me, and the man eventually became drunk and fell asleep. God opened the door, and I ran through it! While trying to find my way home, I saw a man standing by a payphone. He saw me crying and offered to help. I walked with him until he led me toward a dark alley, and I sensed a voice tell me to run. It was God again. I ran onto a highway and held my thumb out to catch a ride quickly, and a man on his way home from a party picked me up. I was relieved until he coerced me into a sexual exchange for the ride.

When I got home, I fell on my face in tears. I knew that God had answered my prayer and brought me back alive. Today I am a happy wife and mother of a beautiful adult daughter. Though I may never fully understand why I was sexually violated that night, it doesn't matter. What happened to me didn't shame me then, and it does not shame me now. My faith in Jesus Christ saved my life that night. Since then, Jesus has shown me that I am clean, worthy, loved and blameless regardless of what I did while under coercion. There is no condemnation in Jesus. There is nothing too awful we can do that He will not forgive. Jesus makes all things new. He did it for me, and I know He will do it for you! That's how much He loves us.

That's why we can be so sure that every detail in our lives of love for God is worked into something good.

—Romans 8:28

48

Dear God, thank You for loving me no matter what I've done and no matter what has been done to me. Teach me how to put my faith in You Lord. Shield me from harm intended to keep me from living out the purpose You had for my life when You created me. Your word says I am worth far more than even the finest gems of the earth, and I am clothed with strength and dignity. Please help me to embrace these words of truth today.

MY FEET ARE GROUNDED AND MY HEAD IS LIFTED HIGH!

I AM FORGIVEN AND BLAMELESS.

I AM SHIELDED BY FAITH.

TODAY, I WILL TRADE MY DOUBT

FOR HIS PROTECTION.

I AM PRICELESS!

But you, Lord, are a shield around me...

Psa 3:3

You are **SECURE**

At day's end I'm ready for sound sleep, for you, God, have put my life back together.

—Psalm 4:8

TRADE YOUR FEAR FOR HIS SECURITY

I didn't want to be here. A mom with young children so far, far away from friends and family with little or no support. Alone. I felt so alone. What if we had a crisis and I needed help? Who would I call? What would I do? Nothing about the current situation was familiar or comfortable. I felt like a tightrope-walker working without a net. Have you ever felt that way?

One night I felt like I had been pushed off my tightrope. I raced to the emergency room following the ambulance that my son was riding in. We had no idea what had happened, but we did know that blue and unresponsive was not normal. Then came days of tests and appointments, words and diagnoses, all while my stomach was in knots. I was in one of those dreams where you fall and just keep falling.

Then came the "net," the one I didn't think I had. Reluctantly, I went to a Bible study and I reached out to a woman I had just met there. I said to her, "Please pray." I wish I could say that I experienced an instant peace, but that wouldn't be true. However, one day I woke up and realized I wasn't falling. The crisis came, it knocked me off the tightrope and it stayed, but no healing came. However, I began to see how God had him and He had me. I traded my tightrope and "safety net" for the security found in God's arms. There is no better place to be.

Can you relate to my experience? I want to encourage you to see that God is there. He will catch you. He can make you feel secure when all you feel is fear. He is a safe place to be. You can trust Him!

Don't panic. I'm with you. There's no need to fear for I'm your GOD. I'll give you strength. I'll help you. I'll hold you steady, keep a firm grip on you...That's right. Because I, your GOD, have a firm grip on you and I'm not letting go. I'm telling you, "Don't panic. I'm right here to help you."

—Isaiah 41:10 & 13

Heavenly Father, I need to know that You are there to catch me when I fall. I need to remember that You are more than enough in my time of need. Thank You for Your love that never fails.

I AM SECURE. I AM SEEN. I AM COMFORTED.
GOD IS MY SAFETY NET. HE LOVES ME!
IN HIS ARMS I WILL REST SECURE.
TODAY, I WILL TRADE MY
FEAR FOR HIS SECURITY.
I AM PRICELESS!

God
IS
OUR
REFUGE
&
strength
ALWAYS
READY TO
HELP
IN
TIMES
OF
need

Psalms
46:1

You are
COURAGEOUS

Be strong. Take courage. Don't be intimidated. Don't give them a second thought because God, your God, is striding ahead of you. He's right there with you. He won't let you down; he won't leave you.

—Deuteronomy 31:6

TRADE YOUR WEAKNESS FOR HIS STRENGTH

I felt that I was trapped in this endless downward spiral of rejection, shame, guilt and fear. I was wrong! My mother had forced me to leave home when I was fourteen. I was a burden, and she just didn't have the patience or the time for me anymore. Her abusive, alcoholic husband was the center of her (codependent) life, and therefore I was in her way.

She refused to believe me when I told her that he had been molesting me. She said that I was lying and trying to cause problems in her relationship with him. How could she not see the signs? How could she not believe me? I guess I shouldn't have been surprised. She had tried to get rid of me when I was twelve by sending me out of town to a male friend who needed a live-in nanny/housekeeper. At first I was relieved, thinking that someone finally wanted and needed me. Reality quickly set in when he raped me.

So what happens to a young girl at fourteen living in Miami Beach? Trust me when I tell you that whatever you could think in your mind is correct. It became a matter of survival for me. It also became a trap. The trap of trying to fill the emptiness and drown out the guilt and shame with alcohol and drugs. The trap of trying to find love in the arms of a man—any man— who would whisper sweet nothings and promise me the world.

Fast forward a little bit. I never found the "magic pill" or remedy for the rejection. The guilt and shame remained. What I *did find* was a diagnosis of Hepatitis C. It nearly cost me my life, as I was six hours from death. I praise God that He had another plan and I'm thankful for the liver transplant I received. The only way I found hope through it all was in Jesus!

He has another plan for you, too. You are strong. You are courageous. You are not alone, though it may seem like it sometimes. God is aware of everything that you are feeling and He is for you. He wants to see you through it all and set you free from the baggage you carry! Will you accept His open invitation for this?

God is a safe place to hide, ready to help when we need him. We stand fearless at the cliff-edge of doom, courageous in seastorm and earthquake, before the rush and roar of oceans, the tremors that shift mountains. Jacob-wrestling God fights for us, God-of-Angel-Armies protects us.

—Psalm 46:1-3

Heavenly Father, oh, how grateful I am that You, my God, fight for me. I am never alone. Please help me to remember who You are and all that You want to be for my life.

I AM STRONG. I AM COURAGEOUS!
I AM VICTORIOUS IN JESUS! TODAY, I WILL
TRADE MY WEAKNESS FOR HIS STRENGTH.
I AM PRICELESS!

Fear not for I have redeemed you; I HAVE CALLED YOU BY NAME, You are mine

Isaiah 43:1

You are RESCUED

God makes everything come out right; he puts victims back on their feet. He showed Moses how he went about his work, opened up his plans to all Israel. God is sheer mercy and grace; not easily angered, he's rich in love.

—Psalm 103:6–8

TRADE YOUR STRUGGLE FOR HIS SHELTER

I used to have a saying about my life: My first father abandoned me, my second father abused me, and my third father was an alcoholic. Not the greatest start; far from it, actually.

For as long as I can remember, I lived as a victim, running from everything. I was scared, ashamed, and alone. I wanted to escape my life. I tried the party scene and everything it had to offer. I lost myself in the nightclubs and to guys and drugs. I didn't want to live and battled suicidal thoughts daily. I was drowning in my pain and I would have drowned a victim if God hadn't rescued me.

I remember the day I met Maria, a woman full of life who told me about God—how He loved me, and could rescue me from the pain and brokenness in my life. I doubted her at first. But I was drawn to her like a magnet, and I finally agreed to go to a Bible study she held for women who had been sexually abused like me. You see, Maria was a survivor herself, having a background like mine. I wanted what she had, so I finally took the leap and joined her group.

After several months of learning about my value in the eyes of God—how I'm wonderfully made, how He loves me beyond my comprehension, how He loved me so much that He died for me—I made the decision to turn my heart and life over to Jesus. My life has never been the same. He transformed me from a victim to a survivor and "put me back on my feet."

You, too, are valued, loved, and cherished by God. It doesn't matter what has happened to you or what you've done, He can take all of that and turn it around for your good. You just have to go to Him and surrender your pain, trading your struggle for His shelter.

As high as the heaven is over the earth, so strong is his love for those who fear him.

—Psalm 103:11

Dear Father God, I can't believe You would love someone like me. After everything I've been through, after everything I've done, I can't imagine how You could transform this for me. But, I don't want to be a victim any longer. I want You to put me back on my feet. Help me to get to know You and see myself the way You see me.

I AM RESCUED. I AM AN OVERCOMER.
I HAVE A GOD WHO LOVES ME
BEYOND MY COMPREHENSION.
HE WILL HELP ME GET BACK ON MY FEET
AND LIVE IN HIS RESCUING POWER.
TODAY, I WILL TRADE MY
STRUGGLE FOR HIS SHELTER.
I AM PRICELESS!

the Lord will Fight For you you need only to be still.

exodus 14:14

But seek first the kingdom of God and His righteousness, and all these things will be provided for you.

—Matthew 6:33 (HCSB)

TRADE YOUR STRIVING FOR HIS REST

"You can do anything you put your mind to!" says society. Anything short of this is failure to reach your true potential. Only, it doesn't quite work like that. According to the Bible, this isn't even the goal. God never asks us to do this.

I am forever an overachiever, and the middle daughter of a [publicly] critical father. Making my mark on the world, much less in my family, has been the goal since birth. However, each new season, has left me feeling like more and more of a failure. It's not for lack of work or effort, that's for sure. But with each passing day, riddled with futility, it's easy to begin thinking, *What am I doing wrong*? Why has the Lord not "blessed" me with "success," whatever we've dreamt that up to be?

It's crazy and somewhat unavoidable how our family dynamics impose themselves on our view of God. And in turn, we've confused human endorsement with that of our Heavenly Father. This, coupled with society's unfair and unfounded expectations on women, has left us running ourselves ragged, always falling short.

It's only natural to assume that if our lives and circumstances are not taking the shape we thought they would, that we are letting God down. Be encouraged my friend: this is simply not how God works.

God says you're already approved. Your approval came through Jesus. Freedom found in being part of a greater Kingdom, the Kingdom of Jesus Christ, should be first and foremost in our lives and thoughts. Resting in this truth, and sharing it with others, is what true success is all about!

Whatever you do [whatever your task may be], work from the soul [that is, put in your very best effort], as [something done] for the Lord and not for men, knowing [with all certainty] that it is from the Lord [not from men] that you will receive the inheritance which is your [greatest] reward. It is the Lord Christ whom you [actually] serve.
—Colossians 3:23 (AMP)

Dear Heavenly Father, please focus my head and my heart on Kingdom things. Help me forgive others, through Your Spirit. Thank You for the ultimate approval that I have experienced in Jesus Christ, my Lord. May You continually calm my overachieving heart and mind, as I settle into all that You have in store for me.

I AM SUCCESSFUL IN THE LORD.

HE ALONE ADORES ME.

HE TREASURES ME FOR WHO I AM.

I AM APPROVED BY HIS LOVE.

TODAY, I WILL TRADE MY STRIVING FOR HIS REST.

I AM PRICELESS!

I have loved you with an EVERLASTING love.

~JEREMIAH 31:3

God is all mercy and grace—not quick to anger, is rich in love.

—Psalm 145:8

TRADE YOUR SHAME FOR HIS FORGIVENESS

I remember looking at the pink line on the stick, feeling so sick, and nauseated. I cannot be pregnant. I am a single mother, with two young children, in an unstable relationship. I'm barely getting by in my current situation, and I can't imagine managing one more child. There is no support, no childcare, and no insurance.

I felt so alone. Abortion seemed like my only option. My circumstances dictated this choice. I truly believed this was my only choice; I didn't have any hope of things changing, and there was no knight in shining armor coming to my rescue.

I felt like such a failure. At that time, I thought, "How did I get here?" Sometimes, when I would wake up in the morning, I would imagine just for a minute that that wasn't my life. All the regrettable choices and shameful acts that left me feeling unworthy, unforgivable, and unlovable came tumbling down over me.

Only the love of God was strong enough to reach for me underneath all that rubble. His grace and compassion brought me to my knees and then to my feet. That same love is available to you, today, in this very moment. There are women who have lived your life and felt your pain, who desire to bring God's love into your life. We were never meant to do life alone. God has someone in mind for you; someone loving, caring and compassionate, who can walk with you through life's challenges.

I know this is true because I experienced it. When I was sitting at home, sick with shame, at my lowest moment, God brought to mind women I had met four years prior. A woman I had judged, and said I would never become, became the very one I would look for and find. And through that experience I found myself.

He doesn't treat us as our sins deserve, nor pay us back in full for our wrongs. As high as heaven is over the earth, so strong is his love to those who fear him. And as far as sunrise is from sunset, he has separated us from our sins.

—Psalm 103:10–12

God, I know You see me. I need help. I need a real person to cry with, learn from, and look out for my best interests. Someone who loves like You do, without condition, who will accept me just as I am. Please open my heart and eyes today, to recognize the messenger You have sent to me, as I surrender my life to You. I believe I am worthy of a blessed life.

I AM FORGIVEN. I AM LOVED. I AM SOUGHT AFTER.
GOD SEES ME AND HE KNOWS ME.
HE LOVES ME JUST AS I AM.
I AM NEVER ALONE.
TODAY, I WILL TRADE MY SHAME
FOR HIS FORGIVENESS.
I AM PRICELESS!

You made all the delicate, inner parts of my body and knit me together in my mother's womb. Thank you for making me so wonderfully complex! Your workmanship is marvelous—how well I know it. You watched me as I was being formed in utter seclusion, as I was woven together in the dark of the womb.
—Psalm 139:13-16 (NLT)

TRADE YOUR TEARS FOR HIS RESTORATION

I can look back and see how frail, frightened, and fragile I was, yet trying to hold on to my dream family, my husband, our two sons, our home, a dog, and the white picket fence. There would be a high price for that dream!

My life at that time was much different than it is today. I was different. I believed in God but did not have a personal relationship with Him. I felt like God was far away and nowhere to be found. I cried out many times, but because I didn't know Him personally I felt very alone and at the end of my hope!!! It was through the pain of my unhealthy marriage, my eating disorder, and a rape during that time that would eventually lead me to the cross where Jesus saved me.

Life was happening all around me. It was like standing on the sidelines watching everyone participate. I would try to jump in, but then feelings of insignificance would overwhelm me. I was a chameleon trying desperately to fit in and gain the love and acceptance of the one I loved so dearly. I compromised who I was to be what others wanted. My life was out of control! The harder I tried to gain control over my surroundings the further lost I became in anorexia and compulsive in exercise. It consumed my world!

The rape I endured during that time threw me further into deep feelings of unworthiness and insignificance that overpowered me. I felt dirty and damaged! The support I desperately needed was in the form of judgment. What was supposed to be my dream life was a nightmare! I had bought the lies of the enemy. I saw myself through the eyes and ugly words of others, causing me to hate my body, flaws, and who I was. The grip of anorexia was so tight it suffocated my hope of living...BUT GOD!

As I look back, I can see the Lord had been pursing me! I realized that He was right there through it all. My life was forever changed that beautiful day in 1999 when I surrendered my heart to Him. He has restored, transformed, and healed my heart. I am renewed physically, spiritually, and emotionally. He can do all this for you too. You are beautifully and uniquely designed on purpose, *for* a purpose! God wants nothing more than to restore you as His masterpiece.

For we are God's masterpiece. He has created us anew in Christ Jesus, so we can do the good things he planned for us long ago.

—Ephesians 2:10 (NLT)

Dear Father God, thank You for reminding me that You uniquely created me and I am Your masterpiece! I am made new in Christ! Lord, help me to see myself through Your eyes and be quick to replace the lies with Your truths that set me free! I embrace the plan and purpose You have predestined for me and look forward to Your leading in my life.

I AM BEAUTIFUL. I AM UNIQUELY AND INTRICATELY
DESIGNED. GOD HAS A GREAT PURPOSE IN MIND FOR MY LIFE.
TODAY, I WILL TRADE MY TEARS FOR HIS RESTORATION.
I AM PRICELESS!

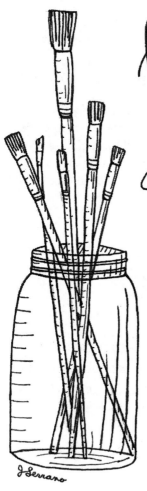

FOR WE ARE GOD'S *handiwork* CREATED IN CHRIST JESUS TO DO *good works,* WHICH GOD PREPARED IN ADVANCE FOR *us to do*

-Ephesians 2:10

For we are God's masterpiece. He has created us anew in Christ Jesus, so we can do the good things he planned for us long ago.

—Ephesians 2:10 (NLT)

TRADE YOUR BLEMISHES FOR HIS WORTH

Masterpiece. You may be reading this and not feel at all that this would describe you. Masterpiece means a person's greatest piece of work, anything done with masterly skill. Now, I totally get how it might be hard to put your name next to that description of yourself. I understand because, for so many years of my life, I found that difficult as well. There are so many things that can happen to us as young girls that can set us on a path that God never intended for us. Things that can shape how we feel about ourselves, that we allow to define us.

Like so many young girls, I was a victim of sexual abuse. It was someone close to me: I remember at the time knowing it was wrong but didn't know what to do with it. I believed the lie for so many years that it must have been my fault. This experience opened so many lies that I would believe for years. Lies that had names, like shame, guilt, and this unending theme that I wasn't good enough.

The day that I met Jesus, in a real authentic way, He shattered all of the lies that I had believed for all those years. He brought me to a place of feeling safe with Him. A place where I could be honest before the God of the universe. You see, I grew up in church but this God I had not met as a young girl. The God that I knew was a God Who was waiting to "hammer" me if I did something wrong. Jesus broke through and showed me that He was safe, that God sees me and cares for me. That I was God's masterpiece, that in Jesus He made me new. The old was gone, a new identity had come, and He was giving me His identity. I learned that He had planned GOOD things for me.

How about you? Do you battle with the question, "Am I enough?" Jesus answers that with an absolute YES! God doesn't make junk; He has made you and He says you are His masterpiece! You are unique and loved. Will you choose to lean in close and allow His truth to replace the lies that you've been believing. You can trust Him with your heart, I promise. I've chosen to trust Him with mine, and it's been an incredible journey to freedom.

Keep me as the apple of your eye; hide me in the shadow of your wings.

—Psalm 17:8 (NIV)

Dear Jesus, I have believed a lot of lies about who I am. Please help me to trade the lies for Your truth about me. I trust You, Jesus, to heal all my hurts and to help me live in the truth that I am enough in You.

I AM ENOUGH. I AM HIS MASTERPIECE.
I AM HIS DAUGHTER, AND MY LIFE HAS
PURPOSE IN JESUS.
TODAY, I WILL TRADE MY
BLEMISHES FOR HIS WORTH.
I AM PRICELESS!

God
is a
safe place
TO HIDE
ready to help
when we need him

Psa 46:1

You are
REDEEMED

Your God is present among you, a strong warrior there to save you. Happy to have you back, he'll calm you with his love and delight you with his songs.

—Zephaniah 3:17

TRADE YOUR GUILT FOR HIS REDEMPTION

I was brought up in a loving home. Loving, but very permissive. I knew my parents loved me unconditionally, but I was rebellious, and got away with whatever I could. I began drinking regularly at 16 because all my friends were, and when I drank, the anxiety I carried around with me disappeared. I puked the first time I drank but the emotional pain outweighed the physical discomfort, so I began to drink every weekend from my sophomore year of high school until I was 29.

I started having sex not long after my drinking became regular, and justified it because I was in a "relationship" for several months and I "loved" him. I would only have sex when I was drunk because I could blame my behavior on the alcohol and my altered state of mind. Once I gave in to my worldly desires, it became easier and easier to have sex in later relationships. I was very ashamed that I was doing this, and never told anyone, even my closest friends.

When I was just 20 and a sophomore in college, I found out I was pregnant. I remember the horror and shame of having to tell my mom and dad. There was no question in any of our minds that I would have an abortion. Although we went to church at times, we were not what you would call a Christ-following family. So, because we had no biblical convictions about it, and having the abortion would make all of our lives "easier," it was scheduled for the following week.

After the procedure, I went back to school like nothing happened. However, deep down, I was traumatized. I did not speak of it again until almost 10 years later. In that time, my drinking increased and my relationships crumbled under the weight of the sorrow and emotional pain I was carrying around.

About nine years later, I finally told someone after becoming a true Christ-follower. The grace and love I felt from people was amazing and so freeing. Mostly, I felt the love and sweet forgiveness from God. I know now how much He cares for me. I still think about my decision often and although I know I am forgiven and fully believe I will see that child in heaven one day, it still affects me. I don't know what guilt you carry, but I do know that God is big enough to carry it for you. He wants to remove your guilt and give you His sweet redemption in place of it. You are dearly loved and nothing you have done can keep God from loving you.

May God himself, the God who makes everything holy and whole, make you holy and whole, put you together—spirit, soul, and body—and keep you fit for the coming of our Master, Jesus Christ. The One who called you is completely dependable. If he said it, he'll do it!

—1 Thessalonians 5:23–24

Dear God, thank You for redemption and the freedom it brings to us emotionally, mentally, and physically. Thank You for Jesus, Who, through His sacrifice, makes us righteous before You.

I AM REDEEMED BECAUSE OF CHRIST'S SACRIFICE.
I AM FORGIVEN AND FREE. I AM LOVED.
TODAY, I WILL TRADE MY GUILT FOR HIS REDEMPTION.
I AM PRICELESS!

HE HAS made EVERYTHING Beautiful IN ITS TIME

ecclesiastes 3:11

©www.Krystalwhitten.com

The Lord appeared to us in the past, saying: "I have loved you with an everlasting love; I have drawn you with unfailing kindness."

—Jeremiah 31:3 (NIV)

TRADE YOUR BROKENNESS FOR HIS WHOLENESS

As a child I was sexually, physically, and emotionally abused. This abuse caused me to develop Complex Post Traumatic Stress Disorder (C-PTSD), a condition that results from long-term exposure to emotional trauma such as emotional, physical, or sexual abuse. I also have Dissociative Identity Disorder (DID), a condition that involves breakdowns of memory, awareness, and identity struggles where there are two or more distinct personality states. In extreme cases, the one personality is unaware of the other. This condition is a result of repeated trauma as a child.

This left me feeling like I was broken—a robot detached from myself and the world. I felt unworthy of any kind of love and because of that, I isolated myself from people. My mental struggles brought me down a path where I would hurt my body by cutting or binge-eating to take the feelings of confusion, numbness, shame, and guilt away for a little while. I felt like King David, a man after the Lord's heart. He felt abandoned, alone and full of despair. David cried out,

"How long, O LORD? Will you forget me forever?"
—Psalm 13:1 (NIV)

Sitting in a fetal position, I broke down and cried out to God, "Help me!" I began to read my Bible and take refuge in Jesus, the only hope that I had left. With time, Bible reading, worshiping, prayer, and working a Christian 12-step recovery program for abused women, I learned God never left me. I learned that my past and my trauma disorder did not define me. I learned that Jesus gives a sound mind and He is not of confusion.

Have you ever felt unworthy? Do you wonder if God is there? I can promise you that He hears your cries. He is ready to help you through this and bring you a greater victory than you could possibly comprehend. When you bring your brokenness to Him, He will replace it with His wholeness. God loves you and He has a beautiful plan for your life!

Is anyone crying for help? God is listening, ready to rescue you. If your heart is broken, you'll find God right there; if you're kicked in the gut, he'll help you catch your breath.

—Psalm 34:17–18

Dear God, I do not always understand your ways, but I do know You are a God of love. Your love was shown to me when Your Son Jesus obediently went to the cross so that I can have a relationship with You, my Father. I surrender the lie that I am broken over to You. Thank You, God, for loving me, and for showing me that I am worthy of Your love.

I AM WORTHY. I AM A WARRIOR AND A CONQUEROR.
I AM WHOLE IN JESUS. I WILL TRUST IN THE LORD.
TODAY, I WILL TRADE MY BROKENNESS
FOR HIS WHOLENESS.
I AM PRICELESS!

So if THE SON sets YOU FREE YoU ARE TRULY FREE

JOHN 8:36

Many of the Samaritans from that village committed themselves to him because of the woman's witness: "He knew all about the things I did. He knows me inside and out!" They asked him to stay on, so Jesus stayed two days. A lot more people entrusted their lives to him when they heard what he had to say. They said to the woman, "We're no longer taking this on your say-so. We've heard it for ourselves and know it for sure. He's the Savior of the world!"

—John 4:39–42

TRADE YOUR PLAN FOR HIS PURPOSE

Screaming in the fetal position in the corner of my bathroom, pulling out my hair just trying to escape the pain within. Words couldn't describe it. Alcohol and drugs only numbed it. Sex took my mind off it. Attempting suicide didn't solve it. Diagnosis and medications couldn't explain it. Hopeless. Helpless. Dark. No purpose. This was my life. Bringing physical pain to myself was the only way I knew how to feel and was reminded I was still living, even though I was actually dying. Walking dead is what I like to call it. Walking through life on the outside but very much dead on the inside.

This is probably how the Samaritan woman felt. Worn out and tired of her lifestyle. Waiting to exhale. Waiting to be rescued. Waiting to find purpose in her life. Jesus came to her in the midst of her daily routine of fetching water from the well. She didn't know that day would be THE DAY her plans would turn into purpose. He invited her into a relationship with Him. Immediately she was awakened. Passion was ignited. So much so that she ran back to her hometown and had to tell them what just happened and who she had just encountered! This woman who felt rejected and burned out on life was CHOSEN to be used by God to set a whole city on fire with purpose and hope and freedom!

At 21 years of age after a second DUI, I found myself in a drug and alcohol treatment facility. As I was checked in, I prayed to myself, "God, who I am coming in is not who I want to be when I leave." It was in my darkest hour that the love of Jesus was so real I tasted something I couldn't get enough of. As I received His forgiveness, shame no longer had a grip on me.

When you give God your pain, He will give you a mighty purpose! He is with you in the darkness, closer than you know. He wants to take your pain and defeat and give you victory!

God's love is meteoric, his loyalty astronomic, his purpose titanic, his verdicts oceanic. Yet in his largeness nothing gets lost; not a man, not a mouse, slips through the cracks.

—Psalm 36:5-6

Father, today I admit I need purpose for my life. I realize it will only be found in the One Who made me. Open my eyes to see, hear, and feel You. Please help me to see that Your plan for my life is one full of purpose!

I AM CHOSEN. I AM LOVED BY JESUS JUST AS I AM.
I AM AN OVERCOMER. I HAVE A VOICE. I WAS BORN TO
MAKE A DIFFERENCE IN THE WORLD.
THERE IS HOPE FOR ME AND
THE PLAN FOR MY LIFE IS ONE FULL OF PURPOSE.
TODAY, I WILL TRADE MY PLAN FOR HIS PURPOSE.
I AM PRICELESS!

Yet I still dare to HOPE.

Lamentations 3:21

This is how we've come to understand and experience love: Christ sacrificed his life for us.

—1 John 3:16

TRADE YOUR REJECTION FOR HIS ACCEPTANCE

You know things are ugly when even your abuser abandons you. Those words "You weren't worth it," "He wants to be with someone else," and even "I never wanted you" actually come to life. How did it come to this? The fears and threats uttered since childhood become the reality and no matter how hard you try to fight, you're left broken, empty, worthless. Did I do this to myself? Or did it start when those who were supposed to love and protect me left?

It doesn't matter if the blame is on me or someone else, I still have a choice to give in and let "them" win or turn to the One Who is bigger than all of this. Isaiah 43:1-3 reads,

"Don't be afraid, I've redeemed you. I've called your name. You're mine. When you're in over your head, I'll be there with you. When you're in rough waters, you will not go down. When you're between a rock and a hard place, it won't be a dead end—Because I am God, your personal God..."

God knows my name. He knows all the details and He promises to be there with me.

1 John 3:1 says that we're called children of God. That means you are royalty because He said so. It's time to start seeing yourself like He sees you. He has called you "His own" and He won't reject Himself. That's not possible. He loved you enough to sacrifice *Himself* for you. Even more, He has precious things to give to you. It's time to start looking past the clouds of what you have known and into the clear future of truth. Today, you have the option to exchange the lies for a new reality. Something beyond yourself that has greater power than any human or entity.

Since God assured us, "I'll never let you down, never walk off and leave you," we can boldly quote, God is there, ready to help; I'm fearless no matter what. Who or what can get to me?

—Hebrews 13:5-6

Dear Jesus, it doesn't make sense but I choose to believe. You see things I can't. I put my trust in You and choose to make Your truth, my reality. You say You love me and will never abandon me, so I'm going to start acting like it. I *am* a daughter of the King. I *am* safe with You. I *can* trust You and know that You will guide and protect me. Help my feelings to follow my choice to depend on You. Help me to feel Your arms around me today. And open my eyes so I can find the numerous ways You are already saying, "I love you."

I AM VALUABLE. I AM WANTED AND BELONG
TO THE ONE WHO MATTERS MOST.
HE LOVED ME ENOUGH TO SACRIFICE HIMSELF FOR ME.
HE WILL TAKE CARE OF ME AND I CAN TRUST HIM.
TODAY, I WILL TRADE MY REJECTION FOR HIS ACCEPTANCE.
I AM PRICELESS!

MIGHTIER

than the

waves of the sea,

the LORD on HIGH

is mighty!

PSALM 93:4

And provide for those who grieve in Zion—to bestow on them a crown of beauty instead of ashes, the oil of gladness instead of mourning, and a garment of praise instead of a spirit of despair. They will be called oaks of righteousness, a planting of the LORD for the display of his splendor.

—Isaiah 61:3 (NIV)

I used to look back on my life and see nothing but ashes. A life destroyed by the choices of others and myself. You see, shame was something I lived with for so long that I didn't know what a life without it looked like. I don't remember when my grandfather started molesting me, but I know I was very young. My grandfather used to tell me I was special, give me little gifts. I thought it was because he loved me, then I found out it was because he wanted to use me. I felt dirty and ashamed that I had allowed the abuse.

I spent my childhood and teen years lashing out in rebellion. Angry at the world. I wasn't happy and I couldn't make the pain go away. I was willing to do anything to feel good, to feel loved, and wanted. I lost my virginity in high school. He told me he loved me and I believed him. When we broke up, I felt used and ashamed. The cycle repeated itself with other boyfriends, and the shame continued to pile on. I started to believe that I would only be loved for my body. There was obviously nothing else to love about me. I went to parties and got drunk, and eventually started doing drugs. There was no pain, no sadness, no shame when I was drunk or high but then I would sober up and it would be back.

By 17 I was pregnant. On Easter Sunday, I went with my dad to the church I had grown up in. I was six-months' pregnant. As I walked in and sat down I was overwhelmingly weighed down by shame. I had heard the Gospel more times than I could count, but something was different that day. The pastor spoke about Jesus, and I sat there sobbing. I was overcome by His love, grace, and mercy. You see, Jesus loves us, right where we are. That love changed me! That love can change you too!

He loved you enough that He laid down His life for you. Your guilt and shame were nailed with Jesus to the cross so that you could have a life of joy. When you surrender your life and your shame to Him, He takes the broken places and gives you His everlasting joy. You don't have to carry those burdens any longer. God longs to heal you and bring beauty out of the ashes of your life.

Instead of their shame my people will receive a double portion, and instead of disgrace they will rejoice in their inheritance; and so they inherit a double portion in their land, and everlasting joy will be theirs.

—Isaiah 61:7 (NIV)

Father God, in Your presence is fullness of joy. You have taken my shame and covered me with Your beautiful grace. When I begin to believe the lie that I am unlovable, help me to remember that Your love is unconditional and *freely* given, not because of anything I do, but because that is Who You are.

I AM WANTED. I AM LOVED AS I AM.
I TRUST THAT GOD WILL BRING BEAUTY
FROM THE ASHES OF MY LIFE.
TODAY, I WILL TRADE MY SHAME FOR HIS JOY.
I AM PRICELESS!

Psalms 27:1

THE LORD
IS
my light
& MY SALVATION
SO
why should I
BE AFRAID?

The Lord
IS MY FORTRESS,
PROTECTING ME
FROM DANGER,
so why should I
TREMBLE?

She said, "Oh sir, such grace, such kindness—I don't deserve it. You've touched my heart, treated me like one of your own. And I don't even belong here!"
—Ruth 2:13

TRADE YOUR GUILT FOR HIS GRACE

Having worked in the sex industry for six years, I had so much shame and guilt. I did so many horrible things that I lost control of my life. I was a horrible person; I did not care about anything and I lost sight of being a mother. I went into the industry on my own, and just got stuck in that life because the money was addicting. In the midst of that, I was searching for love that I never had from my father. I started when I was 19 years old because I thought I wasn't smart enough for school.

Six years later, I ended up in jail for armed drug trafficking, the charges I took for a man I thought loved me. I had so much fear for this man because he had beaten me a couple times that I took the charges so he would not be upset with me. After telling the cops I would take full responsibility for everything, I was facing a minimum of three years in prison.

After a week of realizing this guy was not going to bail me out, I broke down and got on my knees and cried out to God. I just told Him all that had happened in my life and I told Him how sorry I was. God was spiritually operating on my heart in jail. You see, I loved that man so much, and at that point in my life I had given my heart to many men in sacrificial ways that in jail I felt worthless.

With a lot of time to think, I started to read the Bible and pray. I learned that, even through my shame from my sex life, my job, my sins, and these charges, Jesus still loved me. I found out that Jesus looks at me as a beautiful woman who *does* have worth. One day after much thought, I decided to give my life to Jesus and I asked Him to wash all of my sins away. With sincerity, I gave Him my word I would not go back to that life and surrendered my life to Him. It was the most freeing thing I have ever experienced. *God gave me GRACE!* I know if God can give me grace, He can give you grace too, because He loves you so much. God loves you more than any man can ever love you! He gave up His only Son Jesus to die for your freedom.

Jesus said, "Daughter, you took a risk trusting me, and now you're healed and whole. Live well, live blessed!"

—Luke 8:48

Jesus, I'm sorry for all the bad things I have done. Please rewrite my history and make me new. I believe You died for my sins. My shame is here for You to wipe clean. I love You Jesus and I accept You into my life. Thank You for Your grace upon my life.

I AM CHERISHED. I AM BEAUTIFUL.
I AM VALUED. I AM A NEW CREATION
AND MY PAST DOES NOT DEFINE ME.
TODAY, I WILL TRADE MY GUILT FOR HIS GRACE.
I AM PRICELESS!

HE WILL cover you WITH HIS FEATHERS, & under His wings YOU WILL FIND REFUGE HIS faithfulness WILL BE YOUR Shield AND Rampart

Psalm 91:4

Strength and dignity are her clothing, and she smiles at the future.

—Proverbs 31:25 (NASB)

TRADE YOUR DISHONOR FOR HIS HONOR

I was drowning in a sea of disgrace, low self-esteem, insecurity, and self-doubt due to a stigmatizing experience of being branded with a label that did not represent who I was. The shame was unbearable. I became depressed, withdrawn, and didn't want to be around anyone. I mistakenly believed the lies that were being hurled my way.

While deep in my trenches of pity, a beautiful stranger unexpectedly entered my life. This lovely soul noticed me. She recognized my shame and pushed through it with me. She saw beyond the label…she saw *me*.

She saw me through the eyes of Jesus. She saw me with no judgment, but with pure unconditional love. Slowly, I began to understand and believe the truth she was pouring into me. She never gave up as she constantly stood by my side and helped me to remember and reclaim that I am a precious daughter of the King, royalty, a princess, and heir to His eternal throne.

You, too, are royalty. As daughters of the King; we are automatically clothed in a supernatural strength that radiates **dignity, honor, value, and worth**. We are ALWAYS more than "good enough." The evil one wants nothing more than to devour us with his lies by leading us to believe that we are not worthy of the best that life and God has to offer.

It is important to remember the source of our strength is God's strength. The focus of our faith is His faithfulness. The source of our security is His everlasting love. As we go through life, we must never stop learning or growing. God is constantly at work in our lives, patiently molding us and teaching us to become all He wants us to be as His daughters. He promises us strength and grace for every moment and every need…a marvelous, sufficient grace that turns confusion into clarity, doubt into decisiveness, and trouble into triumph.

So, my dear sisters and daughters, in all of our messiness, let's dare to courageously live with a heart wide open, allowing God's light to penetrate the darkness and untangle our ugly web of shame. God sent a beautiful stranger to remind me that His strength and honor is what holds my head high (even if my princess crown is a little crooked). He makes something beautiful and dignified out of our confusion. He disperses our fogginess and allows us to clearly see the beauty and tenderness all around. Such joy!!! It's there for us. It's been there all along! But He has said to me,

My grace is enough; it's all you need.
My strength comes into its own in your weakness.
—2 Corinthians 12:9

Dear Father God, thank You for revealing Your heart of love to me. I embrace who I am in Christ, and now understand that Your power truly is being perfected in my weakness. Lord, please teach me to rely on You. Be my hope, my strength, and my refuge. I forever find favor in Your eyes, in the eyes of the One Who loves me just as I am.

I AM DIGNIFIED. I AM A DAUGHTER OF THE KING. I AM HEIR TO HIS THRONE. I AM A PRINCESS OF GREAT DIGNITY, VALUE, AND WORTH. NO MATTER HOW THE WORLD SEES ME, JESUS SEES ME AS HIS BEAUTIFUL AND INTELLIGENT DAUGHTER. I HOLD MY HEAD HIGH! TODAY, I TRADE MY DISHONOR FOR HIS HONOR.
I AM PRICELESS!

to BESTOW on them a
CROWN of beauty
instead of ASHES
the oil of JOY
instead of MOURNING
a garment of
PRAISE instead of a
SPIRIT of DESPAIR
Isaiah 61

You are RENEWED

"...If I can put a finger on his robe, I can get well." The moment she did it...she could feel the change... "Who touched my robe?" He went on asking, looking around to see who had done it. The woman, knowing what had happened, knowing she was the one, stepped up in fear and trembling, knelt before him, and gave him the whole story.

—Mark 5:25–33

TRADE YOUR REGRET FOR HIS RENEWAL

I am a Christian, a mama, and a wife—three things I never thought I'd be. I grew up in a Christian home but turned my back on Jesus by the time I was 20. I didn't believe in marriage, I didn't want children, and I wanted nothing to do with God. I became a camgirl in my early twenties. "You'll make a TON of money!" I was promised. I was broke, desperate, and had no sense of self-worth, so I thought, why not? I could also do it all from the comfort of my bedroom. I would control the men. I'd be in charge. Porn didn't seem so bad when I looked at it that way.

If you would have asked me at any point during the decade I was active in the sex industry if I'd regret anything, I would have proudly and stubbornly said, no, of course not.

But the attention I thrived on was tearing me apart. I was becoming hollow. Numb. Hurt. Angry. Bitter. My relationships were a disaster. My self-esteem was in the gutter. My life was a wreck. At my lowest point, I tried to kill myself. I didn't plan it—it just sort of rushed upon me. All the hope had drained from my world, and suddenly life didn't seem worth living.

By some miracle, I survived. It took me a long time to recover. I became an outcast. Agoraphobic. Afraid to talk to anyone.

In the aftermath, I opened up to my Christian friend, Brandon. He suggested I read the Gospel of John. I figured, why not? I literally have nothing to lose. I can read one book in the Bible.

The Bible said I could be born again. I liked that—I needed it. I started to cry when I thought of my sins and Jesus' offer to take them away from me. I accepted Christ as my Savior and became new. I changed, but the consequences of my past took longer to deal with.

It's been seven years since that moment. Six years ago I married Brandon, the man God used to reach me. We even had a son! The things I thought I'd never want are now the things I hold most dear. Meanwhile, my biggest regrets remain a click away. Every little thing I did or said is out there.

I learned that selling myself mattered, despite my 'whatever' attitude back then. I am worth more than that, and you are, too. When Christ died on the cross, He took every sin away. We just have to accept His sacrifice. There is nothing you've done that can keep you from the love of God! No sin is bigger than His love for you!

And God showed his love for us by sending his only Son into the world, so that we might have life through him. This is what love is: it is not that we have loved God, but that he loved us and sent his Son to be the means by which our sins are forgiven.
—1 John 4:9–10 (GNT)

Dear Heavenly Father, thank You for reminding me that there is no sin You cannot forgive through Your Son, Jesus Christ. Lord, Your love for me leaves me breathless. I strayed so far away yet You embraced me in the ugliness of my sin and restored me to right standing before You. Thank You for the love, grace, and mercy that You have so freely poured out on my life.

I AM RENEWED. I AM WORTHY. I AM FORGIVEN. I HAVE PURPOSE. I WILL CELEBRATE IN THE FRESH START THAT GOD HAS GIVEN ME. TODAY, I WILL TRADE MY REGRET FOR HIS RENEWAL.
I AM PRICELESS!

Strength
DIGNITY
are her Clothing she
laughs at the days to come
Proverbs 31:25

You're beautiful from head to toe, my dear love,
beautiful beyond compare, absolutely flawless.
—Song of Solomon 4:7

TRADE YOUR SCARS FOR HIS AFFECTION

I remember getting up from the dinner table in tears.
Comments about my weight and my looks were made all
throughout the night and I had come to my breaking point.
Bullied at school and bullied at home in some ways. It left me
with a very poor self-image. The comments about my body
had been coming for several years. I took them like a champ,
but inside I was breaking. Breaking at the weight of my own
insecurity. Would I ever measure up? Would I ever be enough?

I carried those insecurities about my body through a good
portion of my life. They say, "sticks and stones may break my
bones, but words will never hurt me." Really, who came up with
that? What were they thinking? The truth is, words hurt.
They pierced my heart like daggers and left me bleeding for
years to come. Those words made me ashamed to be in shorts,

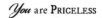

afraid to wear a short-sleeve shirt, fearful of being seen in a bathing suit, always conscious of my body in an unhealthy way.

I looked at myself from the skewed perspective of others' hurtful words. I looked at myself from a broken mirror, you could say. I never really realized how much pain I was in from the words that had been flung my way. Until one day, God revealed how beautiful I am to Him. **He designed me. He knows me. He sees me. He loves me.** He doesn't see what others see. He doesn't have a skewed perspective. As I've grown in my relationship with the Lord, I have come to understand how truly beautiful I am.

But it's not the kind of beauty the world adores. It's a beauty that comes from an identity set on Christ. I walk around more confident now then I've ever been. It's not because I'm a perfect size 4: far from it actually. It's not because I always feel beautiful on the outside. It's because God has helped me see that my value is in Christ alone. I'm cherished. I was worth dying for. I have immense value in Christ. I'm one of a kind. I'm exquisite. I'm gorgeous. I was made in the image of God to reflect His glory, and in that I feel beautiful.

You, my dear, are exquisite. You are stunning. You have beauty inside you that's waiting to be revealed. Your truest beauty can't come into its own until you find your true identity in Christ alone. Embrace the fact that God made you one of a kind. He loves you. He absolutely adores you! He sees no flaw in you. You are truly delightful, my dear!

Those who look to him are radiant; their faces are never covered with shame. —Psalm 34:5 (NIV)

Dear Abba Father, please help me to see that the essence of my beauty is not in makeup, clothing, or how my body was shaped. My beauty comes from who I am in Christ. I was made in the image of God. A child loved, accepted, and adored. You cherish me and call me Your very own. May I live in the splendor of who I am in Your eyes and walk with confidence in the body You have entrusted to me.

I AM RADIANT. I AM BEAUTIFUL. I AM STUNNING IN THE EYES OF GOD. I AM CHERISHED AND TREASURED. HE SEES NOTHING BUT BEAUTY WHEN HE LOOKS AT ME. TODAY, I WILL TRADE MY SCARS FOR HIS AFFECTION. I AM PRICELESS!

Those who look to you
ARE
RADIANT;
their faces are
NEVER COVERED WITH
Shame.

~Psalm 34:5

You are RESTORED

What a God we have! And how fortunate we are to have him, this Father of our Master Jesus! Because Jesus was raised from the dead, we've been given a brand-new life and have everything to live for, including a future in heaven—and the future starts now! God is keeping careful watch over us and the future. The Day is coming when you'll have it all— life healed and whole.

—1 Peter 1:3-5

TRADE YOUR DESPERATION FOR HIS PRESERVATION

I remember that day so well. It was the day I became desperate. Desperate enough to get down on my knees and reach out for the only thing I had the strength to reach for. It had been twelve years that I had dealt with this awful bleeding disease. I was dying. The doctors turned me away, saying there was nothing they could do for me. I spent everything I had to get answers, but the answers didn't come. I didn't want to live like this anymore. Who would? I was ostracized by my community. They didn't want to be around me. They went to the other side of the street when I came near. They stayed as far away from me as possible.

I'm not sure what that solved. It's not like they could have caught my disease. But through the city I was hearing the news of a man who came to town. He was healing people. He was giving the blind sight, He made the lame walk, He gave the deaf hearing, and He stopped to spend time with sinners. Surely this man could heal me.

One day I heard the crowd gathering, and I knew He was coming. Jesus was about to walk by. There were people all around Him, and it seemed nearly impossible to get to Him. But all I needed was the hem of His garment. I got down on my knees and I crawled to my Savior. I reached out to touch the hem of His garment, and instantly I was healed. My healing came from the One who holds the power over life and death. My healing came as I reached out in faith to the One who was there when my mother conceived me.

Yes, that day, that very instant, my bleeding stopped. Healing took place. He turned to me and said, "Daughter, your faith has healed you. Go in peace." (Luke 8:48, NIV) I can't explain to you what I felt when I heard those words. Jesus healed me. I walked away that day a healed woman. No longer bleeding. No longer desperate for healing. I had experienced the healing touch of my Savior. That day forever changed me.

Do you know that Jesus is waiting to heal you? The power that He holds is yours. He just wants you to reach out to Him for it. Are you desperate enough to reach out for His healing touch? Have you tried everything else? Do you know that God has been waiting for you? He wants to bring wholeness to the broken pieces inside your heart. He wants to give you healing. Come experience His healing touch today.

After you have suffered a little while, our God, who is full of kindness through Christ, will give you his eternal glory. He personally will come and pick you up, and set you firmly in place, and make you stronger than ever. —I Peter 5:10 (TLB)

Dear Father God, it continues to astound me that Your Son took on the cross for me. He climbed Calvary's hill with me in mind. He took my sins, my shame and my guilt, and nailed them to the cross. It's by the power of the blood He shed that I experience true and everlasting life.

I AM RESTORED. I AM LOVED AND CHERISHED BY THE KING OF KINGS. I AM FOREVER CHANGED. TODAY, I TRADE MY DESPERATION FOR HIS PRESERVATION. I AM PRICELESS!

(Written by Sarah Malanowski, from the perspective of the bleeding woman mentioned in Luke 8:41-48.)

Cast your cares on the Lord and he will sustain you.

~ Psalm 55:22

Since we've compiled this long and sorry record as sinners (both us and them) and proved that we are utterly incapable of living the glorious lives God wills for us, God did it for us. Out of sheer generosity he put us in right standing with himself. A pure gift. He got us out of the mess we're in and restored us to where he always wanted us to be. And he did it by means of Jesus Christ. —Romans 3:23-24

TRADE YOUR UNWORTHINESS FOR HIS APPROVAL

I stood there ashamed. I knew I was wrong. I knew I deserved death. At least, that's what the law said. I deserved to be stoned. The punishment for my sins was coming. I tensed up, bracing myself for what was to come. I listened to the men around me share my sin. They said, "Teacher, this woman was caught in the act of adultery. In the Law Moses commanded us to stone such women. Now what do you say?" (John 8:4-5, NIV)

I waited for His reply. What would He say to these men? How would He respond? Would He do to me what so many others in the past had done? I waited, but no answer came. The silence was deafening. Jesus was silent. There was no accusation that came from His mouth, no word of admonishment towards me, and no hint of condemnation. He was bent down to the ground, writing something in the sand. As they continued to question Him, He stood and said these words, "If any one of you is without sin, let him be the first to throw a stone at her." (John 8:7, NIV)

I watched these men slowly go away. One by one, they dropped their stones and walked away. The older ones first, then the younger ones. Until the only one left was Jesus. There I was, standing before Jesus in all my shame. I'll never forget His words that day. His words changed my life. They transformed me and gave me a new beginning.

Jesus straightened up and asked *me*, "Woman, where are they? Has no one condemned you?"

"No one, sir," she said.

"Then neither do I condemn you," Jesus declared. "Go now and leave your life of sin."
—John 8:10–11 (NIV, italics mine)

I don't know where you have gotten off track or where sin has wreaked havoc in your life. But I do know the One who forgives sin. I know the One who loves you. He wants to give you a fresh start. He wants you to leave your life of sin and follow Him. There is no greater invitation than the one He offers you today. Will you follow the One who gives true life?

Yes, all have sinned; all fall short of God's glorious ideal; yet now God declares us "not guilty" of offending him if we trust in Jesus Christ, who in his kindness freely takes away our sins.
—Romans 3:23-24 (TLB)

Dear Father God, thank You for declaring "not guilty" on my behalf through Your Son, Jesus. I deserved death for my sins but You sent me a Savior. Lord, may I never forget all that I have been forgiven for. May I live my life to honor You and Your glory as I surrender my failures to Your hands.

I AM FORGIVEN. I AM AFFIRMED. I WILL WALK TALL AND STAND STRONG IN MY LORD. HE SAVED ME FROM THE PENALTY OF MY SINS AND I WILL FOREVER CHERISH THE GIFT OF ETERNAL LIFE I'VE BEEN GIVEN. TODAY, I WILL TRADE MY UNWORTHINESS FOR HIS APPROVAL.
I AM PRICELESS!

(Written by Sarah Malanowski, from the perspective of the woman caught in adultery in John 8:1-11.)

the
love
OF THE LORD REACHES
to the
heavens
and his
faithfulness
TO THE SKIES

Psalms 36:5

You are
SUFFICIENT

Therefore, I tell you, her many sins have been forgiven—for she loved much. But he who has been forgiven little loves little. —Luke 7:47 (NIV)

TRADE YOUR INADEQUACY FOR HIS SUFFICIENCY

I heard that Jesus was going to be at a nearby home, and I knew that I couldn't miss out on the opportunity to meet Him. But I also knew how great the sin was in my life. I knew that I had nothing to offer. I had a heart as sinful as they come. My actions were not pleasing and my thoughts were not honorable. How could I show up to meet Jesus in this condition? I knew the only way I could do it was to humble myself and serve Him. I entered the home with my alabaster jar in hand, ready to pour it out on my could-be Savior. Would He accept me? Would He love me?

I sat there at His feet, weeping, knowing the condition of my own heart and what I had let my life become. He didn't look down on me. I didn't feel His disdain. I never sensed condemnation from Him. All I sensed was love. In fact, the

men in the room had their things to say. They didn't like what I was doing. They made sure to let everyone know just how sinful I really was. But Jesus didn't entertain them for even a minute. In fact, He took the opportunity to share a parable.

I continued to sit there, embracing the moment to wash my Savior's feet. I was drawn into the love I felt pouring out from His heart in the parable. He didn't judge me. He didn't condemn me. He didn't focus on my guilt. He didn't point out my shame. He embraced me. He made me feel sufficient in who I am. I had nothing to offer but my alabaster jar of perfume, my tears that wet His feet, and my hair that dried them. He took what I gave and said it was sufficient. I had enough to give my Master. It was then I heard His voice say, "I tell you her many sins have been forgiven…" (Luke 7:47) Forgiven. I was forgiven. Absolved of all my sins. Jesus, in an instant, took them all!

I've never been the same since. In that moment my life took on purpose. I found that I had something to offer those around me. The scarlet letter of shame I wore walking into the room became my trophy of grace. I walked out of that home a changed woman. Touched by the hand of grace and embraced by the arms of mercy. You, too, can experience this love that I experienced. Jesus has enough to go around. He can and will take your inadequacy and give you sufficiency. You have all you need in Him.

Instead, immense in mercy and with an incredible love, he embraced us. He took our sin—dead lives and made us alive in Christ. He did all this on his own, with no help from us! —Ephesians 2:5

Dear Father God, I look at my sin-stained life and think, *What do I have to bring to You?* Then You gently remind me to bring my heart of service, to lay down my sins at the cross, and to take up the grace and mercy that has captured my heart. Lord, thank You for forgiving me, for not holding my sin against me, and for loving me beyond what I can comprehend. I love You, Lord!

I AM SUFFICIENT. I HAVE ALL I'LL EVER NEED IN JESUS. MY SINS ARE WHITE AS SNOW IN THE PRECIOUS BLOOD HE SHED FOR ME. I'M NOT MY PAST. I'M NOT MY FUTURE. I AM A DAUGHTER OF GOD. CHERISHED BY THE KING OF KINGS, MY HEAVENLY FATHER. TODAY, I WILL TRADE MY INADEQUACY FOR HIS SUFFICIENCY.
I AM PRICELESS!

(Written by Sarah Malanowski, from the perspective of the sinful woman mentioned in Luke 7:36-50.)

For as the heavens are high above the Earth, so great is His steadfast love toward those who fear Him; as far as the East is from the West, so far He removes our transgressions from us.

Psalms 103:11-12

You are EXQUISITE

He has made everything beautiful and appropriate in its time. He has also planted eternity [a sense of divine purpose] in the human heart [a mysterious longing which nothing under the sun can satisfy, except God]—yet man cannot find out (comprehend, grasp) what God has done (His overall plan) from the beginning to the end. —Ecclesiastes 3:11 (AMP)

TRADE YOUR BURDENS FOR HIS FREEDOM

I went to the well that day like any other day. I had learned to go when no one else was around. It didn't matter that the heat of the day was at its hottest. I braved the heat so that I didn't have to face the heat of the people. Yes, they weren't so kind to me. I was a Samaritan, and I didn't have the best reputation. But that day was unlike any other.

I showed up with my bucket in hand, ready to draw water from the well. As I approached the well, the man sitting there asked me for a drink. I was shocked. He was a Jew and I'm a Samaritan. You see, Jews had nothing to do with us

Samaritans. And even further, I was a woman and He was a man. Yet, He talked to me. He asked me for water.

I was a little shocked, and let Him know my thoughts. He expressed the strangest thing to me. He said He could give me living water. I didn't understand how He could do such a thing, as He didn't even have a bucket to draw water with. Where was He going to get this water? He shared with me that anyone who drinks this water would be thirsty again, but the water He gives can be a spring of water welling up to eternal life inside of me. Wow, that amazed me! I wanted this water that He talked about. I didn't want to have to come back to the well any longer, if possible.

Soon our conversation led me to see that this was the Son of God, the Messiah. The One I had been waiting for. He knew all about me. He knew my past. He knew that I had been with five husbands, and that the man I was currently with wasn't my husband. He knew all the ugly things about me, and still talked to me. Even more, He seemed to love me. He made me feel exquisite, like I was worth something. It's hard to explain, but in that moment I felt like I was valued. I had purpose. Jesus saw all of my ugliness and He still loved me.

I did the only sane thing I could do that day: I left my bucket behind and went to share about this man, my Savior. I told my whole town. I left my shame and guilt at the well. I wasn't afraid anymore. I didn't need to hide. I had been given a new lease on life. Someone cared about me. Not just anyone, but the Savior! *My* Savior!

The Savior cares about you, too! There is nothing you could do to make Him love you more. There is nothing you have done that could make Him love you less. He wants to be the Living Water for the thirst in your soul. Will you taste and see that the Lord is good?

So if the Son sets you free, you will be free indeed.
—John 8:36 (NIV)

Lord, I want to experience this freedom I hear about in Your Word. I want to taste the Living Water. Please help me to remember that You don't hold my sin against me. I am forgiven. I am loved. There is nothing I could do to make You love me more. You love me as I am, and continue to teach me who I am in Christ. Thank You for not giving up on me!

I AM EXQUISITE. I HAVE BEEN SET ASIDE WITH PURPOSE. GOD SEES ME. HE LOVES ME. HE KNOWS ME, AND I HAVE EVERYTHING I NEED IN HIM. TODAY, I WILL TRADE MY BURDENS FOR HIS FREEDOM.
I AM PRICELESS!

(Written by Sarah Malanowski, from the perspective of the woman at the well mentioned in John 4:1-42.)

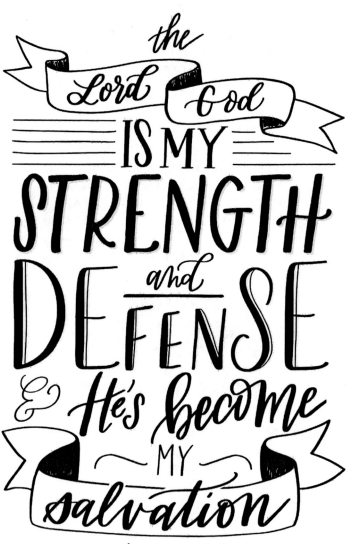

the Lord God IS MY STRENGTH and DEFENSE & He's become MY salvation

isaiah 12:2

You are EMBRACED

After rising from the dead, Jesus appeared early on Sunday morning to Mary Magdalene, whom he had delivered from seven demons. She went to his former companions, now weeping and carrying on, and told them. When they heard her report that she had seen him alive and well, they didn't believe her.

—Mark 16:9–11

TRADE YOUR REJECTION FOR HIS DIGNITY

I walked to the tomb that day, ready to anoint Jesus' body. He had been dead for three days. Never had my heart felt so much grief than during those three days my Savior lay in the grave. He was the One who delivered me from seven demons. I was captured by the spirit of my enemy and essentially dead inside. I was walking around like a zombie, hoping for something more than what I was living. No one had answers for me. No one except Jesus, that is. I'll never forget the day He walked up and delivered me from my tormenters. I'll never forget when He told them that they could not torment me any longer. I was free! I finally felt like I could breathe. I felt like I had a life to live now.

I walked with Jesus very closely after that. I wanted to get as much of Him as I could. I wanted to enjoy His presence and learn from Him. I never really lost my title of the woman whom Jesus delivered of seven demons. I can easily identify with Rahab, the prostitute, and Ruth, the Moabite. Yes, I have a name that's connected to my past. But I've learned that my pain and my past are a trophy of grace in the hands of Jesus. Will you trade in your pain and your past, and allow it to become a trophy of grace in the hands of God? Don't miss out on all He has for you by living one more day in the deadness of your sin.

So as I walked to the tomb, I was reflecting on all of this. I didn't understand why He'd had to die. I didn't fully get it. That day, when I showed up at the tomb and His body was gone, my heart broke. Where was my Savior? Who took Him? What did they do to Him?

As I stood in complete bewilderment, an Angel of the Lord appeared and said to me,

"Do not be afraid, for I know that you are looking for Jesus, who was crucified. He is not here; he has risen, just as he said. Come and see the place where he lay."

—Matthew 28:5–6 (NIV)

In the midst of my agony, someone else caught my attention. I thought He was the gardener. He asked me why I was crying. I didn't recognize Him until I heard Him say my name. In that moment, my eyes opened and I saw my Savior. He was alive. He came to me first. A woman. A woman formerly possessed by seven demons. He came to me. He showed Himself to me. I had felt rejected most of my life; in that moment, I felt dignified. Jesus came to me.

Jesus wants to be your Lord and Savior, too. He knows where you have been. He knows what you have done. He knows how far off-track you have gotten. He doesn't care about all of that. He cares about your heart. He wants you! Will you accept His invitation? Will you come home to Him?

If you want to experience a real relationship with Jesus like I have, please say this prayer…

Dear Father God, I know that I am a sinner. I have nothing to offer you but myself. I know that all my righteous acts are as filthy rags before you. Lord, I know I need Jesus. I need Him to come into my heart and make me a new person. I want to be free. I want to live free. I want to live with purpose and know that I am loved. Lord, please take my brokenness and make me whole in You. Please take the baggage of my life and replace it with Your unending love. Lord, please use the names that have been attached to me and formed my rejection to be trophies of Your grace. Lord, I recognize my need for a Savior and I thank You for dying on the cross for my sins. I want to live for You, as much as I know how to. Please continue to teach me what it means to follow You and love You with all my heart, soul, and strength.

If you said this prayer and want to know more about Jesus, please contact me (Sarah) at sarah@thepricelessjourney.org. I would love to give you some tools to walk out your relationship with the Lord. There is no greater adventure that you can sign up for than the one of living for God and His purpose for your life.

Find a local church that is preaching the Word of God and get involved. Find a small group to get plugged into and make some friends who love Jesus, too. We were never meant to do life alone, so find someone who can encourage you and disciple you in your new walk with Jesus Christ.

Please take a look at our ministry partners in the back of this book and find help for your journey through the resources that they offer you. Also, feel free to join our Facebook community and ask questions. We are here to help you in the journey. You can find our Facebook group at www.facebook.com/groups/youarepriceless.

ALWAYS REMEMBER THESE WORDS...
I AM ADOPTED. I AM FORGIVEN. I AM EMBRACED. I
CAN LIVE BECAUSE JESUS LIVES IN ME. I AM FREE. MY
FREEDOM IS SECURE, AND I'LL LIVE AS A TROPHY OF
GOD'S GRACE. TODAY, I TRADE MY REJECTION FOR
HIS DIGNITY.
I AM PRICELESS!

Because of your new relationship with Jesus you have experienced adoption and now there are many truths that you can apply to your life. As you read the next three devotionals, know that you have a sweet and vibrant identity in Christ.

(Written by Sarah Malanowski, from the perspective of Mary Magdalene in Matthew 28:1-10, Mark 16:1-11, Luke 24:1-12, and John 20:1-18.)

the LORD is my strength and song...

Exodus 15:2

Dear Beloved Daughter,

Today is a new day.[1] I no longer see you from the mistakes you have made. Your past does not define you.[2] You are my beautiful masterpiece.[3] I have begun a work in you that I will be faithful to complete.[4] You, my child are loved with an everlasting love.[5] My love knows no limits. It knows no boundaries. I love you completely and absolutely, and nothing can separate you from my love.[6] I have called you by name.[7] Child you are mine!

When no one wanted you, I wanted you. And through My Son Jesus Christ I have adopted you as My very

1 Lamentations 3:22-23
2 Psalm 103:12
3 Ephesians 2:10
4 Philippians 1:6
5 Jeremiah 31:3
6 Romans 8:38-39
7 Isaiah 43:1

own.[1] I see beauty in you. My treasure. My precious jewel. My beautiful pearl.[2] I see it all when I see you because I see you through My Son now.[3]

The blessings I promise in My Word are yours. I desire to be your comfort, refuge, and safety.[4] Please run to Me when you feel broken and I will make you whole.[5] When you run out of resources, please know that I will provide for you.[6] I am the lover of your soul. I will rescue you, defend you, and restore you. You are truly Mine and I will take care of you.[7]

Come close to Me and I will come close to you.[8] Cling to Me and know that I have nothing but the best in store for your life.[9] When you feel like you are drowning, I will be there to pull you up. When the fires of life get hot, I'll be there to protect you.[10]

I know you may feel weak right now. That's okay! I want to be your strength. My power is truly made

1 Ephesians 1:4-5
2 Deuteronomy 7:6
3 Ephesians 2:4
4 Psalm 62:5-8
5 1 Thessalonians 5:23-24
6 Philippians 4:19
7 Nahum 1:7
8 James 4:8
9 Romans 8:28
10 Isaiah 43:2

perfect in your weakness![1] Always remember, that with Me by your side you are more than a conqueror.[2] And when you lack the strength to fight, please know that I will be fighting for you![3]

I love you, My daughter, and I am setting up eternity for you.[4] You have an eternal home with Me that can't compare to your life on earth.[5] One day, you will join Me in the place that I have prepared for you, a place with no suffering, no sorrow, no pain, and no more sickness.[6]

Truly every tear will be wiped from your eye as you step into your eternal destiny.[7] I'll be waiting for you, My precious daughter!

Loving You Forever,
Your Heavenly Father

1   2 Corinthians 12:9
2   Romans 8:37
3   Exodus 14:14
4   John 14:2
5   2 Corinthians 5:1
6   Revelation 21:4
7   Revelation 7:17

And we know
that for those who
♥
God
all things work
~ together ~
for good

Rom 8:28

My Identity in Christ Jesus

I am bought by the precious blood of Jesus.

(Ephesians 2:13; 1 Corinthians 6:20)

I am redeemed. (Ephesians 1:7; Deuteronomy 7:6)

I am loved. (1 John 4:10)

I am treasured. (1 John 3:1)

I am cherished. (Zephaniah 3:17)

I am a princess of the King. (Romans 8:17)

I am a daughter to my spiritual Father.

(Romans 8:14, 15; Galatians 3:26)

I am blameless and free from accusation. (Colossians 1:22)

I am made complete in Christ. (Colossians 2:10)

I am chosen by God, holy and dearly loved.

(Colossians 3:12; 1 Thessalonians 1:4)

I am a holy partaker of a heavenly calling. (Hebrews 3:1)

I am a member of a chosen race and a royal
  priesthood. (1 Peter 2:9-10)

I am forgiven. (1 John 2:12)

I am a child of God. (1 John 3:1-2; John 1:12)

I am the salt of the earth. (Matthew 5:13)

I am the light of the world. (Matthew 5:14)

I am part of the true vine. (John 15:1, 5)

I am clean. (John 15:3)

I am Christ's friend. (John 15:15)

I am chosen and appointed by God to bear
  His fruit. (John 15:16)

I am free forever from guilt and condemnation.
  (Romans 8:1)

I am adopted. (Galatians 4:4-5)

I am free from sin. (Romans 6:22)

I am a joint heir with Christ. (Romans 8:17)

I am more than a conqueror through Christ,
  who loves me. (Romans 8:37)

I am bought with a price, I am not my own; I
  belong to God. (1 Corinthians 6:19-20)

I am called. (1 Corinthians 7:17)

I am a member of Christ's Body.

(1 Corinthians 12:27; Ephesians 5:30)

I am victorious through Jesus Christ. (1 Corinthians 15:57)

I am a new creation. (2 Corinthians 5:17)

I am reconciled to God. (2 Corinthians 5:18-19)

I am given strength in exchange for weakness.

(2 Corinthians 12:9-10)

I am Abraham's seed… an heir to the promise.

(Galatians 3:29)

I am blessed. (Ephesians 1:3)

I am chosen. (Ephesians 1:4)

I am forgiven. (Psalm 103:11-14)

I am God's workmanship, His handiwork. (Ephesians 2:10)

I am capable. (Philippians 4:13)

I am rescued. (Colossians 1:13)

I am a citizen of Heaven. (Philippians 3:20)

The LORD is MY LIGHT + MY SALVATION Whom shall I fear?

~Psalm 27:1

I am SAFE

1. He will sustain me. (Psalm 55:22)

2. He will strengthen me. (Psalm 89:21)

3. He will be my refuge. (Psalm 62:5-8)

4. He will rescue me. (Psalm 18:17)

5. He will renew me. (Isaiah 40:31)

6. He will be my confidence. (Proverbs 3:26)

7. He hears my prayers. (2 Chronicles 7:14)

8. He will give me perfect peace. (Isaiah 26:3)

9. He will show me great mercy. (Psalm 103:8-14)

10. He restores my soul. (Psalm 23:2-3)

11. He will keep me safe. (Psalm 91:1-4)

12. He will be my guide. (Psalm 48:14)

13. He is my ever-present help in times of trouble. (Psalm 46:1)

14. He that is in me is greater than he that is in the world.
(1 John 4:4)

15. He will meet all my needs. (Philippians 4:19)

16. He will never leave me or forsake me. (Deuteronomy 31:6)

17. He hears my cries. (Psalm 40:1-3)

18. He will give me rest when I come to Him.

    (Matthew 11:28-30)

19. Nothing can separate me from His love. (Romans 8:37-39)

20. Nothing can remove me from His hand. (Psalm 37:23-24)

21. Nothing is impossible for me when done in His strength.

    (Philippians 4:13)

22. Nothing needs to make me stumble today. (Psalm 119:165)

23. If I seek Him I will find Him. (2 Chronicles 15:2)

24. He has abundant wisdom for me in every situation I face.

    (James 1:5)

25. He has set me free, so I will live free!

    (Galatians 5:1; John 8:36)

26. He has given me abundant life. (John 10:10)

27. God will love me forever and ever. (Psalm 89:28)

28. God will not let me be tempted beyond what I can bear.

    (1 Corinthians 10:13)

29. God will wipe every tear from my eyes. (Revelation 21:3-4)

30. He has a reward for me. (Revelation 22:12)

Resources

The Priceless Journey is a resource center providing people with life-transforming resources such as this book. Please visit us at thepricelessjourney.org to learn more.

On our website you will find:
* Other customized City Editions of this book, You Are Priceless.
* More books to help you navigate through the journey of life.
* Priceless Ambassadors who are sharing their stories on our blog.
* Infomation, links, and map to ministries such as the ones on the following pages.
* A Prayer Community where you can share your prayer requests and praises!
* Video testimonials from some of our contributors in this book.
* Downloadable items from this book such as the You Are Adored, I am Adopted, I Am Safe chapters and Scripture Art.
* A place to order hand stamped jewelry with the word Priceless, Treasured, Cherished, and other words from the devotional titles.
* A place for you to contact us and share how Jesus Christ has rescued you! We are gathering testimonies for more books and would love to include yours.

Join our FaceBook group called You Are Priceless. Together we will embrace God's love and discover our ongoing value in Christ Jesus. It will be a safe place to share your heart and grow in your relationship with the Lord! Here is the link you can use to join us...
www.facebook.com/groups/youarepriceless.

FOR THOSE SEEKING IMMEDIATE HELP

POLARIS PROJECT
FOR A WORLD WITHOUT SLAVERY

If you are in a dangerous position and need help right away, please contact the National Human Trafficking Resource Center. There is someone there who can help you! If you would like to be more involved with the fight against human trafficking, you too can contact the hotline.

Phone: 1-888-373-7888
Hours for Hotline: 24 hours, 7 days a week
Text: 233733 (Text "HELP" or "INFO"). Text Advocates are available to respond Monday-Sunday from 3-11pm EST
Languages: English, Spanish, and 200 more languages
Website: Traffickingresourcecenter.org

Focus on the Family Counseling Line
For needs of an urgent or serious nature, we have a staff of licensed professional counselors who are available to listen, pray, and provide guidance. You can arrange to speak with a counselor at no cost by calling **1-855-771-HELP (4357)** Monday through Friday between 6:00 a.m. and 8:00 p.m. Mountain time. If call volumes are high, it may be necessary for you to leave your name and number for a counselor to return your call. One of them will be in touch just as soon as they are able.

U.S. INSTITUTE AGAINST
HUMAN TRAFFICKING

What do we offer?

The U.S. Institute Against Human Trafficking intends to end human trafficking in the United States through prevention, combating demand, the rescue of victims, and providing safe refuge for the restoration of survivors. Our efforts include creating financially stable and replicable safe homes for sexually-exploited children under the age of 18 across the nation, partnering with local law enforcement, governments, businesses, schools, and community-based organizations to create TraffickingFreeZones ™ and educating about the problem and what can be done to stop it. Our headquarters are located in Tampa, Florida.

Contact Information:

Program: Florida Safe Home Program
Contact: Amanda Corbin, LCMSW
Phone: 1-813-895-3390 Ext. 106
Email: acorbin@usiaht.org

All other inquires:
Contact: Natalie Kehn
Phone: 1-813-895-3390 Ext. 103
Email: nkehn@usiaht.org
Website: Usiaht.org

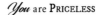

What do we offer?
Selah Freedom is a national organization whose mission is to end sex trafficking and bring freedom to the exploited. Selah Freedom serves those who are 18 and older who are survivors of sex trafficking and exploitation through residential safe housing, which includes a personalized education plan, job placement, medical and legal aid, trauma therapy, mentorship, life skills, and more. Our Outreach Program works on the streets and in the jail system through sex trade support groups bringing resources to survivors. Selah Freedom also provides awareness and teen-prevention programs. Their headquarters are in Sarasota, Florida.

Contact Information:
Phone: 1-888-8-FREE-ME (888-837-3363)
Email: Info@SelahFreedom.com
Website: SelahFreedom.com

To connect with a Salvation Army Anti-Trafficking Program in your area, please contact Dotti. She can help you get connected with Salvation Army Anti-Trafficking programs throughout the nation.

Dotti Groover-Skipper, *Anti-Trafficking Director*
Florida Division, Salvation Army
Email: dotti.groover-skipper@uss.salvationarmy.org
Website: Salvationarmyflorida.org
Office Phone: 813-383-5738   Cell Phone: 813-785-2789

FOR THOSE LOOKING FOR DISCIPLESHIP

THE NAVIGATORS®

The mission of The Navigators is to advance the gospel of Jesus and His Kingdom into the nations through life-on-life mentoring—or discipling—relationships with people, and equipping them to do the same for others. It's what we call "generational multiplication," as the apostle Paul described to his young protégé Timothy: "And the things you have heard me say in the presence of many witnesses entrust to reliable people who will also be qualified to teach others." (2 Timothy 2:2, NIV)

Today, The Navigators is comprised of 11 unique missions, with the aim of helping people know and grow in Jesus Christ on college campuses and military bases, in churches and communities, across the nation and around the world. To learn more about each Navigator Mission you can read its blog about everyday disciple-making. If you would like to request a Navigator to disciple you, use their resources for spiritual growth, and/or see how you can get involved in Navigator ministries, you can go to their website.

Website: Navigators.org

FOR THOSE LOOKING FOR HELP WITH A PREGNANCY

CARE NET.

Care Net envisions a culture where women and men faced with pregnancy decisions are transformed by the gospel of Jesus Christ and empowered to choose life for their unborn children and abundant life for their families. Use our Find a Pregnancy Center tool to locate a center near you!

Website: Care-net.org

HELP SUPPORT THE PRICELESS JOURNEY

Always remember...

For exclusive Priceless products such as this necklace, please visit us at thepricelessjourney.org/shop.

THE Lord IS GOOD a STRONGHOLD in the Midst of TROUBLE

EPILOGUE

How God brought this Book Together

To my dear Priceless One,

Thank you for taking the time to read this book! I pray it
blessed you immensely and that you are walking away from it
with a new sense of who you are in Christ. I pray that you are
encouraged and feel embraced by God's love. I pray that you
will daily embrace the truth found in this book and be renewed
by the mercy of God. There was a lot that went into this book,
so I want to share a little of the background with you. It was a
total God thing that this book came together and daily I rejoice
that He let me be apart of it.

A little over two years ago, God put it on my heart to create a
book for women who are in the commercial sex industry. Not
just that, but it was to be customized for the women of Tampa
Bay. A book custom-designed to reach them right where they
are. I simply put my yes on the table and moved forward in
obedience. I had no idea all that would transpire from that
moment in time when I simply said, "Yes, Lord!"

In July of 2016, I met with my friend Joyce, who is the founder
of the ministry **I Am Freedom Girl**. I knew that she had a
ministry that went into the clubs of Tampa, and I thought she
could help me with this new venture. We sat over coffee at
Starbucks and I shared all that was on my heart. She was quick

to respond and from there we created a list of women we knew who would be a good fit for this project. We were looking for women who had a redemption story where Jesus got a hold of them and brought value to their lives through salvation.

We contacted the women on our list and put together our first meeting. It was a brainstorming session where many of the ideas for this book were formed. We had a sweet time of worship, heard a powerful testimony from someone who had come out of the industry (her story is included in this book), spent time in prayer, and started dreaming of what our book would look like. We were in a place called the Dream Room so it was pretty fitting to spend our time dreaming. We listed all kinds of things. It was in that room that the idea to have trade taglines came to life.

We talked about a title and a cover design. But, honestly, nothing seemed to really click for either of those. All in all, it was a successful meeting; we walked away equipped to start the journey of putting this book together.

During the next several months, God strategically connected me with all kinds of women. Women I had never known or spent time with. It's amazing how every time I spent time with someone I heard a new powerful testimony of God's redeeming work. I'd ask if they would write out their testimony and most said "yes." In fact, one woman you read about in this book shared her testimony for the first time when this book was coming together.

Now, that same woman has grown in courage to share her testimony, and has watched God's redeeming work in something she didn't think had redeeming qualities. She shared her story with me for the second time in her life, and then to a group of us. Each time, she grew in boldness, and I sensed that God was giving her new strength to embrace her testimony fully. It was so beautiful to watch! She is now pursuing a counseling degree to help others who are coming out of the industry.

This happened over and over again as I got to know different women and hear their testimonies. You see, the enemy tries so hard to keep us isolated and thinking that we're the only one this has ever happened to. He makes us think that if we share it we'll be ostracized or looked down on. But honestly, when we expose those things in our hearts, a weight is lifted as we learn we're not alone. There's nothing new under the sun. Whatever your struggle, whatever your battle… I can promise someone has been there before.

We have one of two kingdoms that we can build with our testimonies. In our silence we advance the enemy's kingdom, and in our testifying we advance God's Kingdom. I know it doesn't always look pretty. There are parts of my testimony that I would rather leave tucked away in the back of the closet, but God continues to show me that each part of my testimony was entrusted to me to advance His glory. My ugliness of heart advances the beauty of who He is in me. My weaknesses give room for His strength to be manifested. When I recognize that I can trade my weakness for His strength and my insecurity for

His comfort, then I find true strength! I find my resting place. Yes, in God I have nothing to hide. Everything in my life that has happened or will happen can serve to advance His glory if I let it.

At this time, we still did not have a title for the book or a cover design. I was praying through it, but nothing seemed to work. Then I had one of the devotionals come in from the women with the title, *You Are Priceless.* It clicked right away that this should be the title of the book. At the time, we had no idea of the movie that was coming out or the song that would be written with this title, or even the mural that would be displayed in downtown Tampa. It's so cool looking back, because it was a total God thing! He showed me this would be the title of the book, knowing full well all that was coming out with this Priceless theme attached to it.

About nine months into the project, I got news that my publisher had closed down. It was tough news to hear, and I had no idea what we would do next with this book. But about two weeks prior to this experience the Lord had led me to read Nehemiah. As I read Nehemiah, I felt the Lord was showing me that I needed to stand on the wall. I had no idea what that meant. My marriage was doing well. My children were doing well. From what I could see, I didn't really have a broken-down wall to stand on, yet God called me there, and I acknowledged that's where He wanted me. Later, with the news of my publisher closing down and all the crooked things that they had been doing, I understood why God was calling me to stand on the wall.

God called me to keep pushing forward with this project. To not give up and to trust Him with the outcome! In fact, the Lord had led me to do a number of other things for the book; I followed through on them, still unaware of how the book would take shape or who would publish it.

During this next time frame, God brought in three testimonies from women who'd had abortions. They were a perfect addition to this book. Their testimonies went right along with our stories of redemption.

Another thing that God brought together in this book is the "I am" statements you will see at the end of each devotional. We originally had placed a quote there like I've done in the past with my devotional books, but through a conversation with my friend Christa (a former dancer in the clubs), I learned that these statements would be a better fit. I hope you stopped to look in the mirror and speak each one of these out loud to yourself. Please go back often to these and reflect on who you are in Christ. You are not your past. You are not what you have done. You are so much more in Jesus!

Several delays happened when this book went into the layout stage, but through each delay I learned God had designed something new for this book. God's delays often lead to His most beautiful work when we stay yielded to His Holy Spirit. Through the delay time, I received three extra devotionals for this book, several ministries who jumped on board to be a part of bringing hope to those who read it, and my pastor's foreword. God's delays are often His divine appointments!

If you read through this book and felt a transformation take place in your life, please let us know. We are looking for more testimonies for future editions of this book, as we desire to customize it for cities all across our nation. Your testimony may be the one that's used to bring someone freedom. Please feel free to share your testimony with us at thepricelessjourney.org

Your Priceless Ambassador,

Sarah

Therefore, if anyone is in Christ he is a new creation.

—2 Corinthians 5:17

HELP CUSTOMIZE THIS BOOK FOR YOUR CITY

Every City Edition includes...

1. Testimonies of women from your city. (21 testimonies)
2. A pastoral letter from pastors in your city. (3 pastors)
3. Ministries that are available in your city to help women.
   (5 to 10 ministries)

If you would like to see this book customized for your city, please
contact us at thepricelessjourney.org.

CPSIA information can be obtained
at www.ICGtesting.com
Printed in the USA
FFOW01n1936120318
45533788-46303FF